The Paradoxes of Mr. Pond

G.K. CHESTERTON

WITH A NEW INTRODUCTION BY
MARTIN GARDNER

DOVER PUBLICATIONS, INC.
NEW YORK

Published in Canada by General Publishing Company, Ltd., 30 Lesmill Road, Don Mills, Toronto, Ontario.

Published in the United Kingdom by Constable and Company, Ltd., 10 Orange Street, London WC2H 7EG.

This Dover edition, first published in 1990, is an unabridged republication of the work originally published in London by Cassell and Company Ltd, [1936], and in New York by Dodd, Mead & Company, 1937. A number of typographical errors have been silently corrected in the Dover edition, and a new introduction has been specially written for this edition by Martin Gardner.

Manufactured in the United States of America
Dover Publications, Inc., 31 East 2nd Street, Mineola, N.Y. 11501

Library of Congress Cataloging-in-Publication Data

Chesterton, G. K. (Gilbert Keith), 1874–1936.
    The paradoxes of Mr. Pond / by G.K. Chesterton ; with a new introduction by Martin Gardner.
        p.   cm.
    ISBN 0-486-26185-9
    1. Pond, Mr. (Fictitious character)—Fiction. 2. Detective and mystery stories, English. I. Title. II. Title: Paradoxes of Mister Pond.
PR4453.C4P37 1990
823'.912—dc20   89-11902
                                                                    CIP

INTRODUCTION TO THE DOVER EDITION

IT IS REGRETTABLE that so many loyal fans of Father Brown, Gilbert Keith Chesterton's famous amateur sleuth, are unaware that G. K. wrote five other books of mystery tales that have nothing to do with the little priest. In each of these books the stories are linked together by an unusual device. *The Club of Queer Trades* (a Dover paperback [ISBN 0-486-25534-4] that includes Chesterton's original illustrations) is about members of a London club who earn their living by a trade they each invented. *Four Faultless Felons* (another Dover reprint [ISBN 0-486-25852-1]) tells of four seeming criminals who are actually motivated by high moral objectives. The crime solver in *The Man Who Knew Too Much* is a cynic who knows too much about how modern societies operate. The central character in *The Poet and the Lunatic* is an artist and poet who solves crimes by his ability to feel in himself the motivations behind the behavior of neurotics and psychotics.

The Paradoxes of Mr. Pond is Chesterton's last work of fiction. Seven of its eight stories appeared in the British monthly *Storyteller* in 1935 and 1936. ("The Unmentionable Man" had no prior publication.) After Chesterton died in 1936, the book was published by Cassell and Company. Its ordering of stories is not the same as the order of their appearance in *Storyteller*. "Pond the Pantaloon," for example, is the book's fourth chapter, but was the last to run in the magazine.*

*The original publication dates in *Storyteller* are as follows: "The Three Horsemen of [the] Apocalypse," July 1935; "When Doctors Agree," November; "Ring of Lovers," December; "A Tall Story," February 1936; "The Crime of Captain Gahagan," July; "The Terrible Troubadour," August; "Pond the Pantaloon," September. At least some of the stories appear to have been revised for book publication.

Mr. Pond (we never learn his first name or the color of his hair or eyes) is one of Chesterton's most delightful "detectives." Like Sherlock Holmes's brother Mycroft, Pond works for the British government, though unlike Mycroft he is an obscure bureaucrat in a branch of government that is never made explicit. Chesterton describes him as a "small, neat Civil Servant," a "mild little man" with a domelike forehead (the "brow of Socrates"), and a pointed French beard. When he tugs on his beard it seems to open his mouth like a fish, and his round eyes give him a fishlike or owlish visage. He has a wry sense of humor that prods him into occasional puns. His main hobby is the study of eighteenth-century literature. Mr. Pond knows thoroughly the ways of the world, and his keen mind has an uncanny ability, like the mind of Father Brown, to make shrewd deductions and accurate intuitive guesses.

Pond's most amusing trait—it is what unifies the tales—is his habit of uttering casual remarks that seem to be logical contradictions. They are all the more startling because they occur in the middle of polite, often boring conversation. Indeed, Pond usually talks in a dull monotone, with rare lapses into mild shrillness when he is excited. His conversation is normally as quiet and placid as a pond, we are told, but monsters sometimes swim below a pond's surface and, similarly, in the depths of Pond's memory. They emerge as "monstrous remarks" that make him seem "curious and . . . creepy" and at times utterly mad.

Pond insists that he never intends to utter a paradox—only to state a truism. He is always amazed to discover that someone finds one of his remarks odd. "There's a blind spot on his excellent brain, or a cloud comes over his mind for a moment; and he forgets that he's even said anything peculiar." Each story begins with a Pond statement that wrenches common sense. Pressed for an explanation, he then recounts a bizarre mystery in which he once participated.

> The peculiarity of his conversation was this: in the middle of a steady stream of sense, there would suddenly appear two or three words which seemed simply to be nonsense. It was as if something had suddenly gone wrong with the works of a gramophone. It was nonsense which the speaker never seemed to notice himself; so that sometimes his hearers also hardly noticed that speech so natural was nonsensical. But to those who did notice, he seemed to be saying something like, "Naturally, having no legs, he won the walking-race easily," or "As there was nothing to drink, they all got tipsy at once." Broadly speaking, two kinds of people stopped

him with stares or questions: the very stupid and the very clever. The stupid because the absurdity alone stuck out from a level of intelligence that baffled them; it was indeed in itself an example of the truth in paradox. The only part of his conversation they could understand was the part they could not understand. And the clever stopped him because they knew that, behind each of these queer compact contradictions, there was a very queer story—like the queer story to be narrated here.

All we learn about the book's nameless narrator is on the first page—that Pond was an old friend of his father. Is the narrator Chesterton himself? In the opening paragraph of "When Doctors Agree," G. K. cites a famous paradox of George Bernard Shaw, and another equally famous one by Oscar Wilde. To this he adds a third example, by a "duller scribe": "If a thing is worth doing, it is worth doing badly." The scribe, of course, is Chesterton. He adds that he is now doing penance for earlier vices by celebrating Mr. Pond's virtues. Perhaps he means here only that he is the author of a book in which an imaginary storyteller, not himself, is recording the tales.

Two good friends of Pond figure throughout the book. One is Sir Hubert Wotton, a square-jawed, mustached diplomat well known throughout England. The more colorful friend, Captain Peter Patrick Gahagan, is a large, jovial Roman Catholic Irishman who likes to laugh loudly, especially when Pond uncorks a paradox. Retired from the Army, he has the reputation of a lady-killer and an "irrelevant idler." A great lover of Shakespeare, he enjoys reciting long passages from the plays. Another of his amusing habits is making up tall tales that nobody takes seriously. His role as a foil to Pond is something like the role of Flambeau, the reformed thief in the Father Brown books.

As in all of Chesterton's fiction, there are memorable passages that make even his flimsiest stories a joy to read. Let me single out a few: the discussion of love versus friendship in "The Crime of Captain Gahagan"; the praise of light conversation in "When Doctors Agree"; and the observation in "The Terrible Troubadour" that life is artistic only in spots, never as a whole. In "Pond the Pantaloon," a description of an empty third-class waiting room in a railroad station on a dreary winter day, with its unreadable notices, broken pens, and faded advertisements, is descriptive writing at Chesterton's best.

All of G. K.'s familiar stylistic tricks are here: alliteration, word play, and poetic descriptions of nature's moods. I particularly like these lines:

". . . a space of sunset where the evening clouds passed in a sort of crumbling purple pomp."

". . . faint moonshine that trickled through the cracks between the curtained windows."

"There was a queer, lurid sort of sky over the garden, though there was a fair amount of fitful sunshine almost as capricious as lightning. A huge great mountain of cloud, colored like ink and indigo, was coming up behind the pale, pillared façade of the house, which was still in a wan flush of light."

Some critics have complained that in the last decade of G. K.'s life there was a falling off of creativity, and *The Paradoxes of Mr. Pond* is often held up as proof. In *G. K. Chesterton: A Centenary Appraisal* (1974), edited by John Sullivan, Kingsley Amis calls Pond's paradoxes "irresponsible and pointless mystification." In the same volume, W. W. Robinson excoriates the Pond stories as "childish in a bad sense." (Robinson thinks that the best of Chesterton's non–Father Brown mysteries are those in the collection I consider the worst, *The Man Who Knew Too Much.*) Father Ian Boyd, also writing in Sullivan's anthology, sees in the Pond tales an exaggeration of all the defects he thinks mar G. K.'s earlier stories, especially his reliance on "heavy-handed symbolic details" that have "little relevance to the action they are supposed to illustrate."

I disagree. It is precisely the symbolic details I most enjoy. After all, Chesterton never tried to write realistic fiction, but rather stories that are close to fantasy or to the comic caricatures of Dickens. Actually, there is less symbolism in the Pond stories than in Chesterton's earlier fiction. They are also better plotted and less preposterous than most of his Father Brown yarns, or, for that matter, many of the unlikely adventures of Sherlock Holmes. There may be something to the notion that Chesterton's writing skills declined somewhat in his later years, but in my opinion not much. I rest my case on Chesterton's autobiography, also published posthumously. It is one of his finest and most amusing books. Nor can I detect a hint of decline in the Pond tales. Indeed, I find them more enjoyable than dozens of the later Father Brown stories. Marie Smith, in her introduction to *Thirteen Detectives* (Dodd, Mead, 1987; Penguin, 1989), a collection of Chesterton mysteries that she selected, tells us that Jorge Luis Borges considered "The Three Horsemen of [the] Apocalypse" to be the best of all Chesterton's tales. She quotes his praise of the story's "long white road, white hussars and white horses, and a fascinating struggle of wills."

Father Boyd's animadversions about Pond are harsh and hard to comprehend. In his article in the Sullivan anthology (it is incorporated in Boyd's 1975 book *The Novels of G. K. Chesterton*) Father Boyd does a curious thing. He insists on calling all of G. K.'s short-story collections "novels," then proceeds to fault them for lack of unity! "In *The Paradoxes of Mr. Pond*," Boyd writes, "the breakdown in unity is so complete that instead of a novel one is left with a series of loosely related short stories."

What a strange remark! Of course the Pond book consists of loosely related short stories. That is what they are supposed to be. They are related in the same way that *The Adventures of Sherlock Holmes* are related. Would Father Boyd call *that* book a novel? Actually, Pond's adventures have more unity than Holmes's because, as we have said, their telling is always precipitated by a puzzling paradox which the story illustrates.

Father Boyd is convinced that Pond's adventures also reveal a decline in Chesterton's grasp of politics. This is most noticeable, he writes, in "The Unmentionable Man." The views of the deposed king, Boyd believes, are intended by G. K. to reconcile "the conflicting values of revolutionary Socialism and Liberal idealism." Boyd regards this as too easy a solution to modern political problems, and evidence of Chesterton's "failure of political imagination." He sees the king in this tale as "grim and humorless," not like the flamboyant kings of Chesterton's earlier books. He is a king who has "lost his wit . . . who has learned nothing from experience."

If by "Liberal idealism" Father Boyd means a capitalist free-market economy, then all the world's democratic nations are mixtures of socialism and liberal idealism. Even totalitarian regimes based on the communism of Karl Marx—notably Russia, China, and Yugoslavia—are experimenting with free markets and, let us hope, struggling toward some form of democracy and respect for civil rights. Chesterton's political vision, which he called distributism, was a somewhat formless plan for narrowing the gap between extreme wealth and extreme poverty by a redistribution of land and income. He had little respect for either Marxist socialism or the unregulated free markets of capitalism, seeing distributism as a way of avoiding the evils of both camps. In brief, Chesterton was a democratic socialist, his socialism a mixture (as it is in all democratic societies) of government controls and free enterprise. But aside from all this, and apart from Father Boyd's own political views, it seems to me that he is taking G. K.'s short fiction much too seriously.

Chesterton repeatedly spoke of his mystery stories as light entertainment, adult jokes, games played with the reader. He dashed them off hurriedly to sell to magazines because he needed money, and to bring in additional income when the stories appeared within hard covers. Being a devout Catholic, with a strong philosophical turn of mind, he lifted his mysteries, especially those featuring Father Brown, above the level of mere entertainment by infusing them with philosophical and theological ideas. He was consistently rebuked by non-Christian readers for injecting too much Catholic rhetoric into his fiction. Perhaps this is one reason why such rhetoric is minimal in the Pond series. Exceptions are in "When Doctors Agree," where Chesterton indulges in his lifelong dislike of Calvinism, and in "The Terrible Troubadour," where he allows Pond to make old and naive attacks on evolution.

G. K. would, I believe, have roared with laughter had he read Father Boyd's complaints about lack of unity in his "novel" about Mr. Pond, and Boyd's ponderous attack on the sad, eccentric king who is in a story mainly to provide an outlandish plot and to justify the point of a paradox. If you must read political theory into this tale, consider the recently deceased Hirohito, emperor of Japan. Millions of Japanese were ashamed of him, but they could not deport him because of the sentimental fondness of so many Japanese for the ways of their ancestors. A large portion of the population of today's England look upon the Royal Family as a joke, and an expensive one at that, but it will be a long time before England will manage to rid itself of symbolic kings and queens, and all the ridiculous pomp and conspicuous waste that envelop them. The point of Chesterton's story is that cultures with a long monarchial tradition do not easily abandon their monarchs, and sometimes a king or queen may hold more enlightened political views—feel more compassion for the poor—than the elected hacks who actually control a nation.

I have often wondered why *Storyteller* declined "The Unmentionable Man." Perhaps the editors thought it subtly dishonored both Crown and Parliament. To me it is one of the best and funniest tales in the book. It reminds me of Lord Dunsany's fantasy "The Exiles Club," in which deposed kings are servants of the forgotten gods of Greece. I am not sure, but at times I fancy that Chesterton intended his threadbare monarch to symbolize the King of Kings—a king who, at the time Chesterton wrote, had already become unmentionable in British politics, but a man the nation could not banish. On the other hand, I may be making the same mistake as Father Boyd: searching too hard for ulterior motives in a yarn intended as little more than lighthearted comedy.

Martin Gardner

Hendersonville, North Carolina

CONTENTS

The Paradoxes of
Mr. Pond

THE THREE HORSEMEN
OF APOCALYPSE

THE CURIOUS and sometimes creepy effect which Mr. Pond
produced upon me, despite his commonplace courtesy and
dapper decorum, was possibly connected with some memories of
childhood; and the vague verbal association of his name. He was a
Government official who was an old friend of my father; and I fancy
my infantile imagination had somehow mixed up the name of Mr.
Pond with the pond in the garden. When one came to think of it, he
was curiously like the pond in the garden. He was so quiet at all
normal times, so neat in shape and so shiny, so to speak, in his
ordinary reflections of earth and sky and the common daylight. And
yet I knew there were some queer things in the pond in the garden.
Once in a hundred times, on one or two days during the whole year,
the pond would look oddly different; or there would come a flitting
shadow or a flash in its flat serenity; and a fish or a frog or some more
grotesque creature would show itself to the sky. And I knew there were
monsters in Mr. Pond also: monsters in his mind which rose only for a
moment to the surface and sank again. They took the form of
monstrous remarks, in the middle of all his mild and rational
remarks. Some people thought he had suddenly gone mad in the
midst of his sanest conversation. But even they had to admit that he
must have suddenly gone sane again.

Perhaps, again, this foolish fantasy was fixed in the youthful mind
because, at certain moments, Mr. Pond looked rather like a fish
himself. His manners were not only quite polite but quite conven-

1

tional; his very gestures were conventional, with the exception of one occasional trick of plucking at his pointed beard which seemed to come on him chiefly when he was at last forced to be serious about one of his strange and random statements. At such moments he would stare owlishly in front of him and pull his beard, which had a comic effect of pulling his mouth open, as if it were the mouth of a puppet with hairs for wires. This odd, occasional opening and shutting of his mouth, without speech, had quite a startling similarity to the slow gaping and gulping of a fish. But it never lasted for more than a few seconds, during which, I suppose, he swallowed the unwelcome proposal of explaining what on earth he meant.

He was talking quite quietly one day to Sir Hubert Wotton, the well-known diplomatist; they were seated under gaily-striped tents or giant parasols in our own garden, and gazing towards the pond which I had perversely associated with him. They happened to be talking about a part of the world that both of them knew well, and very few people in Western Europe at all: the vast flats fading into fens and swamps that stretch across Pomerania and Poland and Russia and the rest; right away, for all I know, into the Siberian deserts. And Mr. Pond recalled that, across a region where the swamps are deepest and intersected by pools and sluggish rivers, there runs a single road raised on a high causeway with steep and sloping sides: a straight path safe enough for the ordinary pedestrian, but barely broad enough for two horsemen to ride abreast. That is the beginning of the story.

It concerned a time not very long ago, but a time in which horsemen were still used much more than they are at present, though already rather less as fighters than as couriers. Suffice it to say that it was in one of the many wars that have laid waste that part of the world—in so far as it is possible to lay waste such a wilderness. Inevitably it involved the pressure of the Prussian system on the nation of the Poles, but beyond that it is not necessary to expound the politics of the matter, or discuss its rights and wrongs here. Let us merely say, more lightly, that Mr. Pond amused the company with a riddle.

"I expect you remember hearing," said Pond, "of all the excitement there was about Paul Petrowski, the poet from Cracow, who did two things rather dangerous in those days: moving from Cracow and going to live in Poznan; and trying to combine being a poet with being a patriot. The town he was living in was held at the moment by the Prussians; it was situated exactly at the eastern end of the long causeway; the Prussian command having naturally taken care to hold the bridgehead of such a solitary bridge across such a sea of swamps. But their base for that particular operation was at the western end of the causeway; the celebrated Marshal Von Grock was in general command; and, as it happened, his own old regiment, which was still his favourite regiment, the White Hussars, was posted nearest to the beginning of the great embanked road. Of course, everything was spick and span, down to every detail of the wonderful white uniforms, with the flame-coloured baldrick slung across them; for this was just before the universal use of colours like mud and clay for all the uniforms in the world. I don't blame them for that; I sometimes feel the old epoch of heraldry was a finer thing than all that epoch of imitative colouring, that came in with natural history and the worship of chameleons and beetles. Anyhow, this crack regiment of cavalry in the Prussian service still wore its own uniform; and, as you will see, that was another element in the fiasco. But it wasn't only the uniforms; it was the uniformity. The whole thing went wrong because the discipline was too good. Grock's soldiers obeyed him too well; so he simply couldn't do a thing he wanted."

"I suppose that's a paradox," said Wotton, heaving a sigh. "Of course, it's very clever and all that; but really, it's all nonsense, isn't it? Oh, I know people say in a general way that there's too much discipline in the German army. But you can't have too much discipline in an army."

"But I don't say it in a general way," said Pond plaintively. "I say it in a particular way, about this particular case. Grock failed because his soldiers obeyed him. Of course, if *one* of his soldiers had obeyed him, it wouldn't have been so bad. But when *two* of his soldiers obeyed him—why, really, the poor old devil had no chance."

Wotton laughed in a guttural fashion. "I'm glad to hear your new military theory. You'd allow one soldier in a regiment to obey orders; but two soldiers obeying orders strikes you as carrying Prussian discipline a bit too far."

"I haven't got any military theory. I'm talking about a military fact," replied Mr. Pond placidly. "It is a military fact that Grock failed, because two of his soldiers obeyed him. It is a military fact that he might have succeeded, if one of them had disobeyed him. You can make up what theories you like about it afterwards."

"I don't go in much for theories myself," said Wotton rather stiffly, as if he had been touched by a trivial insult.

At this moment could be seen striding across the sun-chequered lawn, the large and swaggering figure of Captain Gahagan, the highly incongruous friend and admirer of little Mr. Pond. He had a flaming flower in his buttonhole and a grey top-hat slightly slanted upon his ginger-haired head; and he walked with a swagger that seemed to come out of an older period of dandies and duellists, though he himself was comparatively young. So long as his tall, broad-shouldered figure was merely framed against the sunlight, he looked like the embodiment of all arrogance. When he came and sat down, with the sun on his face, there was a sudden contradiction of all this in his very soft brown eyes, which looked sad and even a little anxious.

Mr. Pond, interrupting his monologue, was almost in a twitter of apologies: "I'm afraid I'm talking too much, as usual; the truth is I was talking about that poet, Petrowski, who was nearly executed in Poznan—quite a long time ago. The military authorities on the spot hesitated and were going to let him go, unless they had direct orders from Marshal Von Grock or higher; but Marshal Von Grock was quite determined on the poet's death; and sent orders for his execution that very evening. A reprieve was sent afterwards to save him; but as the man carrying the reprieve died on the way, the prisoner was released, after all."

"But as——" repeated Wotton mechanically.

"The man carrying the *reprieve,*" added Gahagan somewhat sarcastically.

"Died on the way," muttered Wotton.

"Why then, of course, the prisoner was released," observed Gahagan in a loud and cheerful voice. "All as clear as clear can be. Tell us another of those stories, Grandpapa."

"It's a perfectly true story," protested Pond, "and it happened exactly as I say. It isn't any paradox or anything like that. Only, of course, you have to know the story to see how simple it is."

"Yes," agreed Gahagan. "I think I should have to know the story, before realizing how simple it is."

"Better tell us the story and have done with it," said Wotton shortly.

Paul Petrowski was one of those utterly unpractical men who are of prodigious importance in practical politics. His power lay in the fact that he was a national poet but an international singer. That is, he happened to have a very fine and powerful voice, with which he sang his own patriotic songs in half the concert halls of the world. At home, of course, he was a torch and trumpet of revolutionary hopes, especially then, in the sort of international crisis in which practical politicians disappear, and their place is taken by men either more or less practical than themselves. For the true idealist and the real realist have at least the love of action in common. And the practical politician thrives by offering practical objections to any action. What the idealist does may be unworkable, and what the man of action does may be unscrupulous; but in neither trade can a man win a reputation by doing nothing. It is odd that these two extreme types stood at the two extreme ends of that one ridge and road among the marshes—the Polish poet a prisoner in the town at one end, the Prussian soldier a commander in the camp at the other.

For Marshal Von Grock was a true Prussian, not only entirely practical but entirely prosaic. He had never read a line of poetry himself; but he was no fool. He had the sense of reality which belongs to soldiers; and it prevented him from falling into the asinine error of the practical politician. He did not scoff at visions; he only hated them. He knew that a poet or a prophet could be as dangerous as an army. And he was resolved that the poet should die. It was his one compliment to poetry; and it was sincere.

He was at the moment sitting at a table in his tent; the spiked helmet that he always wore in public was lying in front of him; and his massive head looked quite bald, though it was only closely shaven. His whole face was also shaven; and had no covering but a pair of very strong spectacles, which alone gave an enigmatic look to his heavy and sagging visage. He turned to a Lieutenant standing by, a German of the pale-haired and rather pudding-faced variety, whose blue saucer-eyes were staring vacantly.

"Lieutenant Von Hocheimer," he said, "did you say His Highness would reach the camp to-night?"

"Seven forty-five, Marshal," replied the Lieutenant, who seemed rather reluctant to speak at all, like a large animal learning a new trick of talking.

"Then there is just time," said Grock, "to send you with that order for execution, before he arrives. We must serve His Highness in every way, but especially in saving him needless trouble. He will be occupied enough reviewing the troops; see that everything is placed at His Highness's disposal. He will be leaving again for the next outpost in an hour."

The large Lieutenant seemed partially to come to life and made a shadowy salute. "Of course, Marshal, we must all obey His Highness."

"I said we must all serve His Highness," said the Marshal.

With a sharper movement than usual, he unhooked his heavy spectacles and rapped them down upon the table. If the pale blue eyes of the Lieutenant could have seen anything of the sort, or if they could have opened any wider even if they had, they might as well have opened wide enough at the transformation made by the gesture. It was like the removal of an iron mask. An instant before, Marshal Von Grock had looked uncommonly like a rhinoceros, with his heavy folds of leathery cheek and jaw. Now he was a new kind of monster: a rhinoceros with the eyes of an eagle. The bleak blaze of his old eyes would have told almost anybody that he had something within that was not merely heavy; at least, that there was a part of him made of steel and not only of iron. For all men live by a spirit, though it were an evil spirit, or one so strange to the commonalty of Christian men that they hardly know whether it be good or evil.

"I said we must all serve His Highness," repeated Grock. "I will speak more plainly, and say we must all save His Highness. Is it not enough for our kings that they should be our gods? Is it not enough for them to be served and saved? It is we who must do the serving and saving."

Marshal Von Grock seldom talked, or even thought, as more theoretical people would count thinking. And it will generally be found that men of his type, when they do happen to think aloud, very much prefer to talk to the dog. They have even a certain patronizing relish in using long words and elaborate arguments before the dog. It would be unjust to compare Lieutenant Von Hocheimer to a dog. It would be unjust to the dog, who is a much more sensitive and vigilant creature. It would be truer to say that Grock in one of his rare moments of reflection, had the comfort and safety of feeling that he was reflecting aloud in the presence of a cow or a cabbage.

"Again and again, in the history of our Royal House, the servant has saved the master," went on Grock, "and often got little but kicks for it, from the outer world at least, which always whines sentimentalism against the successful and the strong. But at least we were successful and we were strong. They cursed Bismarck for deceiving even his own master over the Ems telegram; but it made that master the master of the world. Paris was taken; Austria dethroned; and we were safe. To-night Paul Petrowski will be dead; and we shall again be safe. That is why I am sending you with his death-warrant at once. You understand that you are bearing the order for Petrowski's instant execution—and that you must remain to see it obeyed?"

The inarticulate Hocheimer saluted; he could understand that all right. And he had some qualities of a dog, after all: he was as brave as a bulldog; and he could be faithful to the death.

"You must mount and ride at once," went on Grock, "and see that nothing delays or thwarts you. I know for a fact that fool Arnheim is going to release Petrowski to-night, if no message comes. Make all speed."

And the Lieutenant again saluted and went out into the night; and mounting one of the superb white chargers that were part of the splendour of that splendid corps, began to ride along the high, narrow road along the ridge, almost like the top of a wall, which overlooked the dark horizon, the dim patterns and decaying colours of those mighty marshes.

Almost as the last echoes of his horse's hoofs died away along the causeway, Von Grock rose and put on his helmet and his spectacles and came to the door of his tent; but for another reason. The chief men of his staff, in full dress, were already approaching him; and all along the more distant lines there were the sounds of ritual salutation and the shouting of orders. His Highness the Prince had come.

His Highness the Prince was something of a contrast, at least in externals, to the men around him; and, even in other things, something of an exception in his world. He also wore a spiked helmet, but that of another regiment, black with glints of blue steel; and there was something half incongruous and half imaginatively appropriate, in some antiquated way, in the combination of that helmet with the long, dark, flowing beard, amid all those shaven Prussians. As if in keeping with the long, dark, flowing beard, he wore a long, dark, flowing cloak, blue with one blazing star on it of the highest Royal Order; and under the blue cloak he wore a black uniform. Though as German as any man, he was a very different kind of German; and something in his proud but abstracted face was consonant with the legend that the one true passion of his life was music.

In truth, the grumbling Grock was inclined to connect with that remote eccentricity the, to him, highly irritating and exasperating fact that the Prince did not immediately proceed to the proper review and reception by the troops, already drawn out in all the labyrinthine parade of the military etiquette of their nation; but plunged at once impatiently into the subject which Grock most desired to see left alone: the subject of this infernal Pole, his popular-

ity and his peril; for the Prince had heard some of the man's songs
sung in half the opera-houses of Europe.

"To talk of executing a man like that is madness," said the Prince,
scowling under his black helmet. "He is not a common Pole. He is a
European institution. He would be deplored and deified by our allies,
by our friends, even by our fellow-Germans. Do you want to be the
mad women who murdered Orpheus?"

"Highness," said the Marshal, "he would be deplored; but he
would be dead. He would be deified; but he would be dead. Whatever
he means to do, he would never do it. Whatever he is doing, he
would do no more. Death is the fact of all facts; and I am rather fond of
facts."

"Do you know nothing of the world?" demanded the Prince.

"I care nothing for the world," answered Grock, "beyond the last
black and white post of the Fatherland."

"God in heaven," cried His Highness, "you would have hanged
Goethe for a quarrel with Weimar!"

"For the safety of your Royal House," answered Grock, "without
one instant's hesitation."

There was a short silence and the Prince said sharply and suddenly:
"What does this mean?"

"It means that I had not an instant's hesitation," replied the
Marshal steadily. "I have already myself sent orders for the execution
of Petrowski."

The Prince rose like a great dark eagle, the swirl of his cloak like the
sweep of mighty wings; and all men knew that a wrath beyond mere
speech had made him a man of action. He did not even speak to Von
Grock; but talking across him, at the top of his voice, called out to the
second in command, General Von Voglen, a stocky man with a
square head, who had stood in the background as motionless as a
stone.

"Who has the best horse in your cavalry division, General? Who is
the best rider?"

"Arnold Von Schacht has a horse that might beat a racehorse,"
replied the General promptly. "And rides it as well as a jockey. He is
of the White Hussars."

"Very well," said the Prince, with the same new ring in his voice.
"Let him ride at once after the man with this mad message and stop
him. I will give him authority, which I think the distinguished
Marshal will not dispute. Bring me pen and ink."

He sat down, shaking out the cloak, and they brought him writing materials; and he wrote firmly and with a flourish the order, overriding all other orders, for the reprieve and release of Petrowski the Pole.

Then amid a dead silence, in the midst of which old Grock stood with an unblinking stare like a stone idol of prehistoric times, he swept out of the room, trailing his mantle and sabre. He was so violently displeased that no man dared to remind him of the formal reviewing of the troops. But Arnold Von Schacht, a curly-haired active youth, looking more like a boy, but wearing more than one medal on the white uniform of the Hussars, clicked his heels, and received the folded paper from the Prince; then, striding out, he sprang on his horse and flew along the high, narrow road like a silver arrow or a shooting star.

The old Marshal went back slowly and calmly to his tent, slowly and calmly removed his spiked helmet and his spectacles, and laid them on the table as before. Then he called out to an orderly just outside the tent; and bade him fetch Sergeant Schwartz of the White Hussars immediately.

A minute later, there presented himself before the Marshal a gaunt and wiry man, with a great scar across his jaw, rather dark for a German, unless all his colours had been changed by years of smoke and storm and bad weather. He saluted and stood stiffly at attention, as the Marshal slowly raised his eyes to him. And vast as was the abyss between the Imperial Marshal, with Generals under him, and that one battered non-commissioned officer, it is true that of all the men who have talked in this tale, these two men alone looked and understood each other without words.

"Sergeant," said the Marshal, curtly, "I have seen you twice before. Once, I think, when you won the prize of the whole army for marksmanship with the carbine."

The sergeant saluted and said nothing.

"And once again," went on Von Grock, "when you were questioned for shooting that damned old woman who would not give us information about the ambush. The incident caused considerable comment at the time, even in some of our own circles. Influence, however, was exerted on your side. My influence."

The sergeant saluted again; and was still silent. The Marshal continued to speak in a colourless but curiously candid way.

"His Highness the Prince has been misinformed and deceived on a point essential to his own safety and that of the Fatherland. Under this error, he has rashly sent a reprieve to the Pole Petrowski, who is to be executed to-night. I repeat: who is to be executed to-night. You must immediately ride after Von Schacht, who carried the reprieve, and stop him."

"I can hardly hope to overtake him, Marshal," said Sergeant Schwartz. "He has the swiftest horse in the regiment, and is the finest rider."

"I did not tell you to overtake him. I told you to stop him," said Grock. Then he spoke more slowly: "A man may often be stopped or recalled by various signals: by shouting or shooting." His voice dragged still more ponderously, but without a pause. "The discharge of a carbine might attract his attention."

And then the dark sergeant saluted for the third time; and his grim mouth was again shut tight.

"The world is changed," said Grock, "not by what is said, or what is blamed or praised, but by what is done. The world never recovers from what is done. At this moment the killing of a man is a thing that must be done." He suddenly flashed his brilliant eyes of steel at the other, and added: "I mean, of course, Petrowski."

And Sergeant Schwartz smiled still more grimly; and he also, lifting the flap of the tent, went out into the darkness and mounted his horse and rode.

The last of the three riders was even less likely than the first to indulge in imaginative ideas for their own sake. But because he also was in some imperfect manner human, he could not but feel, on such a night and such an errand, the oppressiveness of that inhuman landscape. While he rode along that one abrupt ridge, there spread out to infinity all round him something a myriad times more inhuman than the sea. For a man could not swim in it, nor sail boats on it, nor do anything human with it; he could only sink in it, and practically without a struggle. The sergeant felt vaguely the presence of some primordial slime that was neither solid nor liquid nor capable of any form; and he felt its presence behind the forms of all things.

He was atheist, like so many thousands of dull, clever men in Northern Germany; but he was not that happier sort of pagan who can see in human progress a natural flowering of the earth. That world before him was not a field in which green or living things evolved and developed and bore fruit; it was only an abyss in which all living things would sink for ever as in a bottomless pit; and the thought hardened him for all the strange duties he had to do in so hateful a world. The grey-green blotches of flattened vegetation, seen from above like a sprawling map, seemed more like the chart of a disease than a development; and the land-locked pools might have been of poison rather than water. He remembered some humanitarian fuss or other about the poisoning of pools.

But the reflections of the sergeant, like most reflections of men not normally reflective, had a root in some subconscious strain on his nerves and his practical intelligence. The truth was that the straight road before him was not only dreary, but seemed interminably long. He would never have believed he could have ridden so far without catching some distant glimpse of the man he followed. Von Schacht must indeed have the fleetest of horses to have got so far ahead already; for, after all, he had only started, at whatever speed, within a comparatively short time. As Schwartz had said, he hardly expected to overtake him; but a very realistic sense of the distances involved had told him that he must very soon come in sight of him. And then, just as despair was beginning to descend and spread itself vaguely over the desolate landscape, he saw him at last.

A white spot, which slightly, slowly, enlarged into something like a white figure, appeared far ahead, riding furiously. It enlarged to that extent because Schwartz managed a spurt of riding furiously himself; but it was large enough to show the faint streak of orange across the white uniform that marked the regiment of the Hussars. The winner of the prize for shooting, in the whole army, had hit the white of smaller targets than that.

He unslung his carbine; and a shock of unnatural noise shook up all the wild fowl for miles upon the silent marshes. But Sergeant Schwartz did not trouble about them. What interested him was that, even at such a distance, he could see the straight, white figure turn crooked and alter in shape, as if the man had suddenly grown deformed. He was hanging like a humpback over the saddle; and Schwartz, with his exact eye and long experience, was certain that his victim was shot through the body; and almost certain that he was shot through the heart. Then he brought the horse down with a second shot; and the whole equestrian group heeled over and slipped and slid and vanished in one white flash into the dark fenland below.

The hard-headed sergeant was certain that his work was done. Hard-headed men of his sort are generally very precise about what they are doing; that is why they are so often quite wrong about what they do. He had outraged the comradeship that is the soul of armies; he had killed a gallant officer who was in the performance of his duty;

he had deceived and defied his sovereign and committed a common murder without excuse of personal quarrel; but he had obeyed his superior officer and he had helped to kill a Pole. These two last facts for the moment filled his mind; and he rode thoughtfully back again to make his report to Marshal Von Grock. He had no doubts about the thoroughness of the work he had done. The man carrying the reprieve was certainly dead; and even if by some miracle he were only dying, he could not conceivably have ridden his dead or dying horse to the town in time to prevent the execution. No; on the whole it was much more practical and prudent to get back under the wing of his protector, the author of the desperate project. With his whole strength he leaned on the strength of the great Marshal.

And truly the great Marshal had this greatness about him: that after the monstrous thing he had done, or caused to be done, he disdained to show any fear of facing the facts on the spot or the compromising possibilities of keeping in touch with his tool. He and the sergeant, indeed, an hour or so later, actually rode along the ridge together, till they came to a particular place where the Marshal dismounted, but bade the other ride on. He wished the sergeant to go forward to the original goal of the riders, and see if all was quiet in the town after the execution, or whether there remained some danger from popular resentment.

"Is it here, then, Marshal?" asked the sergeant in a low voice. "I fancied it was further on; but it's a fact the infernal road seemed to lengthen out like a nightmare."

"It is here," answered Grock, and swung himself heavily from saddle and stirrup, and then went to the edge of the long parapet and looked down.

The moon had risen over the marshes and gone up strengthening in splendour and gleaming on dark waters and green scum; and in the nearest clump of reeds, at the foot of the slope, there lay, as in a sort of luminous and radiant ruin, all that was left of one of those superb white horses and white horsemen of his old brigade. Nor was the identity doubtful; the moon made a sort of aureole of the curled golden hair of young Arnold, the second rider and the bearer of the reprieve; and the same mystical moonshine glittered not only on baldrick and buttons, but on the special medals of the young soldier and the stripes and signs of his degree. Under such a glamorous veil of light, he might almost have been in the white armour of Sir Galahad; and there could scarcely have been a more horrible contrast than that between such fallen grace and youth below and the rocky and grotesque figure looking down from above. Grock had taken off his helmet again; and though it is possible that this was the vague shadow of some funereal form of respect, its visible effect was that the queer naked head and neck like that of a pachyderm glittered stonily in the moon, like the hairless head and neck of some monster of the Age of Stone. Rops, or some such etcher of the black, fantastic German schools, might have drawn such a picture: of a huge beast as inhuman as a beetle looking down on the broken wings and white and golden armour of some defeated champion of the Cherubim.

Grock said no prayer and uttered no pity; but in some dark way his mind was moved, as even the dark and mighty swamp will sometimes move like a living thing; and as such men will, when feeling for the first time faintly on their defence before they know not what, he tried to formulate his only faith and confront it with the stark universe and the staring moon.

"After and before the deed the German Will is the same. It cannot be broken by changes and by time, like that of those others who repent. It stands outside time like a thing of stone, looking forward and backward with the same face."

The silence that followed lasted long enough to please his cold vanity with a certain sense of portent; as if a stone figure had spoken in a valley of silence. But the silence began to thrill once more with a distant whisper which was the faint throb of horsehoofs; and a moment later the sergeant came galloping, or rather racing, back along the uplifted road, and his scarred and swarthy visage was no longer merely grim but ghastly in the moon.

"Marshal," he said, saluting with a strange stiffness, "I have seen Petrowski the Pole!"

"Haven't they buried him yet?" asked the Marshal, still staring down and in some abstraction.

"If they have," said Schwartz, "he has rolled the stone away and risen from the dead."

He stared in front of him at the moon and marshes; but, indeed, though he was far from being a visionary character, it was not these things that he saw, but rather the things he had just seen. He had, indeed, seen Paul Petrowski walking alive and alert down the brilliantly illuminated main avenue of that Polish town to the very beginning of the causeway; there was no mistaking the slim figure with plumes of hair and tuft of Frenchified beard which figured in so many private albums and illustrated magazines. And behind him he had seen that Polish town aflame with flags and firebrands and a population boiling with triumphant hero-worship, though perhaps less hostile to the government than it might have been, since it was rejoicing at the release of its popular hero.

"Do you mean," cried Grock with a sudden croaking stridency of voice, "that they have dared to release him in defiance of my message?"

Schwartz saluted again and said:

"They had already released him and they have received no message."

"Do you ask me, after all this," said Grock, "to believe that no messenger came from our camp at all?"

"No messenger at all," said the sergeant.

There was a much longer silence, and then Grock said, hoarsely: "What in the name of hell has happened? Can you think of anything to explain it all?"

"I have seen something," said the sergeant, "which I think does explain it all."

When Mr. Pond had told the story up to this point, he paused with an irritating blankness of expression.

"Well," said Gahagan impatiently, "and do *you* know anything that would explain it all?"

"Well, I think I do," said Mr. Pond meekly. "You see, I had to worry it out for myself, when the report came round to my department. It really did arise from an excess of Prussian obedience. It also arose from an excess of another Prussian weakness: contempt. And of all the passions that blind and madden and mislead men, the worst is the coldest: contempt.

"Grock had talked much too comfortably before the cow, and much too confidently before the cabbage. He despised stupid men even on his own staff; and treated Von Hocheimer, the first messenger, as a piece of furniture merely because he looked like a fool; but the Lieutenant was not such a fool as he looked. He also understood what the great Marshal meant, quite as well as the cynical sergeant, who had done such dirty work all his life. Hocheimer also understood the Marshal's peculiar moral philosophy: that an act is unanswerable even when it is indefensible. He knew that what his commander wanted was simply the corpse of Petrowski; that he wanted it anyhow, at the expense of any deception of princes or destruction of soldiers. And when he heard a swifter horseman behind him, riding to overtake him, he knew as well as Grock himself that the new messenger must be carrying with him the message of the mercy of the Prince. Von

Schacht, that very young but gallant officer, looking like the very embodiment of all that more generous tradition of Germany that has been too much neglected in this tale, was worthy of the accident that made him the herald of a more generous policy. He came with the speed of that noble horsemanship that has left behind it in Europe the very name of chivalry, calling out to the other in a tone like a herald's trumpet to stop and stand and turn. And Von Hocheimer obeyed. He stopped, he reined in his horse, he turned in his saddle; but his hand held the carbine levelled like a pistol, and he shot the boy between the eyes.

"Then he turned again and rode on, carrying the death-warrant of the Pole. Behind him horse and man had crashed over the edge of the embankment, so that the whole road was clear. And along that clear and open road toiled in his turn the third messenger, marvelling at the interminable length of his journey; till he saw at last the unmistakable uniform of a Hussar like a white star disappearing in the distance, and he shot also. Only he did not kill the second messenger, but the first.

"That was why no messenger came alive to the Polish town that night. That was why the prisoner walked out of his prison alive. Do you think I was quite wrong in saying that Von Grock had two faithful servants, and one too many?"

THE CRIME OF
CAPTAIN GAHAGAN

IT MUST BE CONFESSED that some people thought Mr. Pond a bore. He had a weakness for long speeches, not out of self-importance, but because he had an old-fashioned taste in literature; and had unconsciously inherited the habit of Gibbon or Butler or Burke. Even his paradoxes were not what are called brilliant paradoxes. The word brilliant has long been the most formidable weapon of criticism; but Mr. Pond could not be blasted and withered with a charge of brilliancy. Thus, in the case now to be considered, when Mr. Pond said (referring, I grieve to say, to the greater part of the female sex, at least in its most modern phase): "They go so fast that they get no farther," he did not mean it as an epigram. And somehow it did not sound epigrammatic; but only odd and obscure. And the ladies to whom he said it, notably the Hon. Violet Varney, could see no sense in it. They thought Mr. Pond, when he was not boring, was only bewildering.

Anyhow, Mr. Pond did sometimes indulge in long speeches. Triumph therefore and great glory belongs to anyone who could successfully stop Mr. Pond from making long speeches; and this laurel is for the brows of Miss Artemis Asa-Smith, of Pentapolis, Pa. She came to interview Mr. Pond for *The Live Wire*, touching his alleged views on the Haggis Mystery; and she did not let him get a word in edgeways.

"I believe," began Mr. Pond, rather nervously, "that your paper is inquiring about what some call Private Execution, and I call murder, but——"

"Forget it," said the young lady briefly. "It's just too wonderful for me to be sitting here next to all secrets of your government; why——" She continued her monologue; though in a style of dots and dashes. As she would not let Mr. Pond interrupt her, she seemed to think it only fair to interrupt herself. Somehow it seemed at once as if her speech would never end; and not one sentence of it was ever ended.

We have all heard of American interviewers who rip up family secrets, break down bedroom doors and collect information in the manner of burglars. There are some; but there are also others. There are, or were, when the writer remembers them, a very large number of intelligent men ready to discuss intelligent things; and there was Miss Asa-Smith. She was small and dark; she was rather pretty and would have been very pretty if she had not dipped her lipstick in hues of earthquake and eclipse. Her finger-nails were painted five different colours, looking like the paints in a child's paintbox; and she was as innocent as a child. She was also as garrulous as a child. She felt something paternal about Mr. Pond and told him everything. He did not have to tell her anything. No buried tragedies of the Pond family were dug up; no secrets of the crimes committed behind Mr. Pond's bedroom door. Conversation, so to describe it, revolved largely round her early days in Pennsylvania; her first ambitions and ideals; which two things, like many of her local traditions, she seemed to imagine to be the same. She was a Feminist and had stood up with Ada P. Tuke against clubs and saloons and the selfishness of man. She had written a play; and she just longed to read it to Mr. Pond.

"About that question of Private Execution," said Mr. Pond politely, "I suppose we've all been tempted in desperate moments——"

"Well, I'm just desperate to read you this play, and—you know how it is. You see, my play's awfully *modern*. But even the modernest people haven't done just that—I mean, beginning in the water and then——"

"Beginning in the water?" inquired Mr. Pond.

"Yes, isn't it just too—oh, you know. I suppose they will have all characters in bathing dresses soon—but they'll only just enter L. or R.; come on at the side, you know—and all the old stuff. My characters enter from above, diving, with a splash—— Well, that'll be a splash, won't it? I mean to say, it begins like that." She began to read very rapidly:

"*Scene,* sea outside the Lido.

"Voice of Tom Toxin (*from above*): 'See me make a splash, if——'

(*Toxin dives from above to stage in pea-green bathing-suit*).

"Voice of Duchess (*from above*): 'Only sort of splash you'll ever make, you——' (*Duchess dives from above in scarlet bathing-suit*).

"Toxin (*coming up spluttering*): 'Splutter as splutter . . . splosh is the only splash by your——.'

"Duchess: 'Oh, Grandpa!' "

"She calls him Grandpa, you see, because 'splosh' means money in that ever-so-old comic song—they're quite young really, of course, and rather . . . you know. But——"

Mr. Pond interposed with delicacy and firmness: "I wonder whether you would be so very kind, Miss Asa-Smith, as to leave the manuscript with me or send me a copy, so that I can enjoy it at leisure. It reads rather quickly for old buffers like me; and nobody ever seems to finish a sentence. But do you think you can persuade our leading actors and actresses to dive from great heights into a stage sea?"

"Oh, I dare say some of the old-stagers would be stuffy about it," she replied, "because—can't fancy your great tragedienne, Olivia Feversham—though she's not so old really and just lovely still, only—but so Shakespearian! But I've got the Honourable Violet Varney to *promise,* and her sister's quite a friend of mine, though of course not so—and lots of amateurs would do it for fun. That Gahagan guy is a good swimmer, and he's acted, too, and—oh, well, he'd click if Joan Varney's in it."

The face of Mr. Pond, hitherto patient and stoical, became quite silently alert and alive. He said with a new gravity:

"Captain Gahagan is a great friend of mine, and he has introduced me to Miss Varney. As to her sister, the one on the stage——"

"Not a patch on Joan, is she? But——" said Miss Asa-Smith.

Mr. Pond had formed an impression. He liked Miss Asa-Smith. He liked her very much. And the thought of the Honourable Violet Varney, that English aristocrat, made him like the American even more. The Honourable Violet was one of those wealthy women who pay to act badly; and blackleg the poorer people who might have been paid to act well. She certainly was quite capable of diving in a bathing dress, or in anything or nothing, if it were the only way to the stage and the spot-light. She was quite capable of helping Miss Asa-Smith in her absurd play and talking similar nonsense about being modern and independent of selfish man. But there was a difference; and it was not to the advantage of the Honourable Violet. Poor Artemis followed idiotic fashions because she was a hard-working journalist who had to earn her living; and Violet Varney only took away other people's living. They both spoke in the style that was a string of unfinished sentences. It was the one language Mr. Pond thought that might truly be called broken English. But Violet dropped the tail of a sentence as if she were too tired to finish it; Artemis did so as if she were really too eager to get on to the next. There was within her, somehow, a thing, a spirit of life, which survives every criticism of America.

"Joan Varney's much nicer," continued Artemis, "and you bet your friend Gahagan thinks so. Do you think they'll really hitch up? He's a queer fellow, you know."

Mr. Pond did not deny it. Captain Gahagan, that swaggering and restless and sometimes sullen man-about-town, was queer in many ways; and in none more than in his almost incongruous affection for the precise and prosaic Mr. Pond.

"Some say he's a rotter," said the candid American. "I don't say that; but I do say he's a dark horse. And he does shilly-shally about Joan Varney, doesn't he? Some say he's really in love with the great Olivia—your only tragic actress. Only she's so jolly tragic."

"God send she doesn't play in a real tragedy," said Pond.

He knew what he meant; but he had not the faintest foreshadowing of the awful tragedy of real life and death in which Olivia Feversham was to play within the next twenty-four hours.

He was only thinking of his Irish friend as he knew him; and he was near enough to know all that he did not know. Peter Patrick Gahagan lived the modern life, perhaps to excess, was a prop of nightclubs and a driver of sports cars, still comparatively young; but, for all that, he was a survival. He belonged to the times of a more Byronic pose. When Mr. W. B. Yeats wrote: "Romantic Ireland's dead and gone; it's with O'Leary in the grave," he had never met Gahagan, who was not yet in the grave. He was of that older tradition by a hundred tests; he had been a cavalry soldier and also a member of Parliament; the last to follow the old Irish orators with their rounded periods. Like all these, for some reason, he adored Shakespeare. Isaac Butt filled speeches with Shakespeare; Tim Healy could quote the poet so that his poetry seemed part of the living talk at table; Russell of Killowen read no other book. But he, like they, was Shakespearian in an eighteenth-century way: the way of Garrick; and that eighteenth century that he recalled had a pretty pagan side to it. Pond could not dismiss the chances of Gahagan having an affair with Olivia or anyone else; and if so a storm might be brewing. For Olivia was married; and to no complaisant husband, either.

Frederick Feversham was something worse than an unsuccessful actor; he was one who had been successful. He was now forgotten in the theatre and remembered only in the law-courts. A dark and crabbed man, still haggardly handsome, he had become famous, or familiar, as a sort of permanent litigant. He was eternally bringing actions against people whom he charged with trivial tricks and distant and disputable wrongs: managers and rivals and the rest. He had as yet no special quarrel with his wife, younger than himself and still popular in the profession. But he was much less intimate with his wife than with his solicitor.

Through court after court Feversham passed, pursuing his rights and followed like a shadow by his solicitor, Luke, of the firm of Masters, Luke and Masters; a young man with flat, yellow hair and a rather wooden face. What he thought of his client's feuds and how far he ventured to restrain them, that wooden face would never reveal. But he worked well for his client; and the two had necessarily become in a way companions-in-arms. Of one thing Pond was certain. Neither Feversham nor Luke was likely to spare Gahagan, if that erratic gentleman put himself in the wrong. But this part of the problem was destined to find a worse solution than he dreamed of. Twenty-four hours after Pond's talk with the interviewer, he learned that Frederick Feversham was dead.

Like other litigious persons, Mr. Feversham had left a legal problem behind him, to feed many lawyers with fees. But it was not the problem of an ill-drawn will or a dubious signature. It was the problem of a stiff and staring corpse, lying just inside a garden-gate and nailed there by a fencing-sword with the button broken off. Frederick Feversham, that legalist, had suffered at least one final and indisputable illegality; he had been stabbed to death as he entered his own home.

Long before certain facts, slowly collected, were put before the police, they were put before Mr. Pond. This may seem odd, but there were reasons; indeed Mr. Pond, like many other Government officials, had rather secret and unsuspected spheres of influence; his public powers were very private. Younger and more conspicuous men had even been known to stand in a certain awe of him, owing to special circumstances. But to explain all that is to explore the labyrinth of the most unconstitutional of all constitutions. In any case, his first warning of the trouble took the commonplace form of an ordinary legal letter, with the heading of the well-known firm of

Masters, Luke and Masters, expressing the hope that Mr. Luke might be allowed to discuss certain information with Mr. Pond, before it was necessary for it to reach the police authorities or the Press. Mr. Pond replied equally formally that he would be delighted to receive Mr. Luke at a certain hour upon the following day. Then he sat and stared into vacancy, with that rather goggling expression which led some of his friends to compare him to a fish.

He had already thought of about two-thirds of what the solicitor was going to tell him.

"The truth is, Mr. Pond," said the solicitor, in a confidential but still careful voice, when he was at length deposited on the other side of Mr. Pond's table next day. "The truth is that the possibilities of this affair, painful in any case, may be specially painful for you. Most of us find it impossible to imagine that a personal friend might come under suspicion in such matters."

The mild eyes of Mr. Pond opened very wide, and even his mouth made the momentary movement which some thought so very fishy. The lawyer probably assumed that he was shocked at the first suggestion of his friend being affected; in fact, he was mildly amazed to suppose that anybody had not entertained the idea long ago. He knew that words to that effect were common in the more conventional detective stories, which he heartily enjoyed, as a change from Burke and Gibbon. He could see the printed words on a hundred pages: "None of us could believe that this handsome young cricketer had committed a crime," or: "It seemed absurd to connect murder with a man like Captain Pickleboy, the most popular figure in Society." He had always wondered what the words meant. To his simple and sceptical eighteenth-century mind, they seemed to mean nothing at all. Why should not pleasant and fashionable men commit murders, like anybody else? He was very much upset himself, inside, about this particular case; but he still did not understand that way of talking.

"I am sorry to say," continued the lawyer in a low voice, "that private investigation which we have already made, on our own account, places your friend, Captain Gahagan, in a position requiring explanation."

"Yes," thought Pond, "and, my God, Gahagan really does require explanation! That's exactly the difficulty about him—but, Lord, how slow this fellow is!" In short, the real trouble was that Pond was very fond of Captain Gahagan; but in so far as one could ask whether men were capable of murder, he was rather inclined to think that Gahagan *was* capable of murder—more capable of murder than of meanness to a cabman.

Suddenly, with extraordinary vividness, the image of Gahagan himself sprang up in Pond's memory: Gahagan as he had last seen him lounging with his large shoulders and long stride, and strange dark-red hair under the rather rakishly tilted grey top-hat, and behind him a space of sunset where the evening clouds passed in a sort of crumbling purple pomp, rather like the pomp of poor Gahagan himself. No; the Irishman was a man seventy-and-seven times to be forgiven; but not a man to be lightly acquitted.

"Mr. Luke," said Pond suddenly, "will it save time if I tell you, to start with, what I know there is against Gahagan? He was hanging round Mrs. Feversham, the great actress; I don't know why he was; my own belief is that he is really in love with another woman. Yet he did unquestionably give the actress a huge amount of his time: hours and hours and late hours too. But if Feversham caught him doing anything unconventional, Feversham was not the man to let him off without a lawsuit and a scandal and God knows what. I don't want to criticize your client; but, speaking crudely, he almost lived on lawsuits and scandals all his life. And if Feversham was the man to threaten or blackmail, I give it you frankly that Gahagan was the man to hit him back in a bodily fashion; and perhaps kill him, especially if a lady's name were involved. That is the case against Captain Gahagan; and I tell you at the start that I don't believe in it."

"Unfortunately it is not the whole case against Captain Gahagan," replied Luke smoothly, "and I fear the full statement may make even you believe it. Perhaps the most serious result of our investigations is this. It is now quite clearly established that Captain Gahagan gave three quite contrary and inconsistent accounts of his movements, or proposed movements, on the evening of the murder. Allowing him the highest possible marks for truthfulness in the matter, he must at least have told two lies to one truth."

"I have always found Gahagan truthful enough," replied Pond, "except when he was telling lies for amusement; which is really rather the mark of a man who doesn't prostitute the sublime art of lying to the base uses of necessity. About all ordinary practical things, I have found him not only frank but also rather precise."

"Even accepting what you say," answered Mr. Luke dubiously, "we should still have to answer: If he was commonly candid and truthful, it must have been a mortal and desperate occasion that made him lie."

"To whom did he tell these lies?" asked Pond.

"That is where the whole matter is so painful and delicate," said the lawyer, shaking his head. "That afternoon, it seems, Gahagan had been talking to several ladies."

"He generally has," said Pond. "Or was it they who were talking to him? If one of them happened, for instance, to be that very charming lady, Miss Asa-Smith of Pentapolis, I would venture to guess that it was she who was talking to him."

"This is rather extraordinary," said Luke in some surprise. "I do not know if it was a guess; but one of them certainly was a Miss Asa-Smith of Pentapolis. The other two were the Hon. Violet Varney and, last but not least, the Hon. Joan Varney. As a matter of fact, it was the last that he spoke to first; which, I suppose, was only natural. It is notable, on your own suggestion, that he is really attached to this last lady, that his statement to her was apparently much the nearest to the truth."

"Ah," said Mr. Pond, and pulled his beard thoughtfully.

"Joan Varney," observed the lawyer gravely, "stated most definitely, before she knew that there was any trouble or tragedy in this case, that Captain Gahagan had left the house saying: 'I am going round to the Fevershams'.' "

"And you say that is contradicted by his statement to the others," said Mr. Pond.

"Most emphatically," replied Luke. "The other sister, well known on the stage as Violet Varney, stopped him as he was going out and they exchanged a little light conversation. But, as he left, he distinctly said to her: 'I'm not going to the Fevershams'; they're still at Brighton,' or something like that."

"And now we come," said Mr. Pond, smiling, "to my young friend from Pentapolis. What was she doing there, by the way?"

"He found her on the doorstep when he opened the front door," replied Mr. Luke, also smiling. "She had arrived in a rush of enthusiasm to interview Violet Varney as 'Comedienne and Social Leader.' Neither she nor Gahagan are the sort of people not to be noticed; or to fail to notice each other. So Gahagan had a little talk with her, too; at the end of which he departed, with a flourish of his grey top-hat, telling her that he was going immediately to the club."

"Are you certain of that?" asked Pond, frowning.

"She was certain of it; because she was in a red-hot rage about it," replied Luke. "It seems that she has some feminist fad on the subject. She thinks all male persons who go to clubs go there to tell slanderous anecdotes about women and then drink themselves under the table.

She may have had a little professional feeling about it too; perhaps she would have liked to have a longer interview, either for herself or *The Live Wire*. But I'll swear she's quite honest."

"Oh, yes," said Mr. Pond emphatically but rather gloomily, "she's absolutely honest."

"Well, there it is," said Luke, speaking also not without a decent gloom. "It seems to me that the psychology's only too obvious under the circumstances. He blurted out where he was really going to the girl he was accustomed to confide in; perhaps he didn't really plan the crime till later; or perhaps it wasn't entirely planned or premeditated. But by the time he talked to less friendly people he saw how unwise it would be to say he was going to the Fevershams'. His first impulse is to say, hastily and too crudely, that he was *not* going to the Fevershams'. Then, by the third interview, he thinks of a really good lie, normal and sufficiently vague, and says he is going to the club."

"It might be like that," replied Pond, "or it might——" And Mr. Pond fell for the first time into the lax habit of Miss Asa-Smith, and failed to finish his sentence. Instead he sat staring at the distance with his rather goggle-eyed and fish-like gaze; then he put his head on his hands, said apologetically: "Please pardon me if I think for a minute," and buried his bald brows once more.

The bearded fish came to the surface again with a somewhat new expression, and said with a brisk and almost sharp tone:

"You seem very much bent on bringing the crime home to poor Gahagan."

For the first time Luke's features stiffened to hardness, or even harshness. "We naturally wish to bring the murderer of our client to justice."

Pond bent forward and his eyes were penetrating as he repeated: "But you will have it that the murderer was Gahagan."

"I've given you the evidence," said Luke, lowering; "you know the witnesses."

"And yet, oddly enough," said Pond very slowly, "you haven't mentioned the really damning thing against him in the report of those witnesses."

"It's damning enough—what do you mean?" snapped the lawyer.

"I mean the fact that they are *unwilling* witnesses," replied Pond. "It couldn't be a conspiracy. My little Yank is as honest as the day and would never join a conspiracy. He's the sort of man women like. Even Violet Varney likes him. Joan Varney loves him. And yet they all give evidence to contradict him or, at least, show he contradicted himself. And yet they're all wrong."

"What the devil do you mean," cried Luke with sudden impatience, "by saying they're all wrong?"

"They're all wrong about what he said," answered Pond. "Did you ask them if he said anything else?"

"What else is needed?" cried the lawyer, now really angry. "They could all swear he said what I say. Going to the Fevershams'; not going to the Fevershams'; going to some unnamed club—and then bolting down the street so as to leave a lady in a rage."

"Precisely," said Pond. "You say he said three different things. I say he said the same thing to all three. He turned it the other way round and made it the same."

"He turned it the other way round all right," retorted Luke almost viciously. "But if he goes into the witness-box, he'll find out whether the law of perjury says that turning a thing round makes it the same."

There was a pause and then Mr. Pond said serenely:

"So now we know all about the Crime of Captain Gahagan."

"Who says we know all about anything? I don't. Do you?"

"Yes," said Mr. Pond. "The Crime of Captain Gahagan was that he didn't understand women; especially modern women. These men with a vague air of being lady-killers seldom do. Don't you know that dear old Gahagan is really your great-great-grandfather?"

Mr. Luke made a movement as of sudden and sincere alarm; he was not the first man to fancy for a moment that Mr. Pond was mad.

"Can't you see," went on Pond, "that he belongs to the school of the old bucks and beaux who called her 'Woman, Lovely Woman,' and knew nothing whatever about her—to the considerable increase of her power? But how they could pay compliments! 'Stand close about, you Stygian set. . . . ' But perhaps, as you seem to suggest, it is not quite relevant. But you see what I mean by Gahagan being the old sort of lady-killer?"

"I know he's a very old sort of gentleman-killer," cried Luke quite violently, "and that he killed the worthy and greatly wronged gentleman who was my client and friend!"

"You seem a little annoyed," said Mr. Pond. "Have you tried reading Dr. Johnson's *Vanity of Human Wishes?* Very soothing. Believe me, those eighteenth-century writers I wanted to quote are very soothing. Have you read Addison's play about Cato?"

"You appear to be mad," said the lawyer, now positively pale.

"Or again," continued Mr. Pond in a chatty way, "have you read

Miss Asa-Smith's play about the duchess in the bathing-suit? All the sentences curiously cut short—like the bathing-suit."

"Do you mean anything whatever?" asked the lawyer in a low voice.

"Oh, yes, I mean a great deal," replied Pond. "But it takes quite a long time to explain—like the Vanity of Human Wishes. What I mean is this. My friend Gahagan is very fond of those old wits and orators, just as I am; speeches where you have to wait for the peroration; epigrams with the sting in the tail. That's how we first became friends, by both being fond of the eighteenth-century style; balance and antithesis and all that. Now if you have this habit and read, say, the hackneyed lines in *Cato:* "Tis not in mortals to command success; but we'll do more, Sempronius, we'll deserve it'—well, it may be good or bad; but you've got to wait for the end of the sentence; because it begins with a platitude and ends with a point. But the modern sort of sentence never ends; and nobody waits for it to end.

"Now women were always a little like that. It isn't that they don't think; they think quicker than we do. They often talk better. But they don't *listen* so well. They leap so quickly upon the first point; they see so much more in it; and go off in a gallop of inference about it—so that they sometimes don't notice the rest of the speech at all. But Gahagan, being of the other sort, the old oratorical sort, would always end his sentence properly, and be as careful to say what he meant at the end as the beginning.

"I suggest to you, as the barristers say, that what Captain Gahagan really said to Joan in the first case was this: 'I'm going round to the Fevershams'; I don't believe they are back from Brighton yet, but I'll just look in and see. If they're not, I'll go on to the club.' That is what Peter Gahagan said; but that is not what Joan Varney heard. She heard about going to the Fevershams' and felt at once that she knew all about it—far too much about it—to the not unnatural tune of 'He's going to see that woman'; even though his next words were that the woman almost certainly wasn't there. Stuff about Brighton and the club didn't interest her, and she didn't even remember it. Very well, let us go on to the next case. What Gahagan said to Violet Varney was this: 'It's no good going to the Fevershams' really; they're not back from Brighton; but perhaps I'll look in and see; if they're not back, I shall go on to the club.' Violet is much less truthful and careful than Joan; and she was jealous of Olivia herself, but in a much shallower way, Violet supposing herself to be an actress. She also heard the word Feversham and remembered vaguely that he said it was no good going there; that is, that he was not going there. She was pleased at this and condescended to chat with him; but did not condescend to pay any attention whatever to anything else he said.

"Now for the third case. What Gahagan said to Miss Artemis Asa-Smith on the doorstep was this: 'I'm going to the club; I promised to look in on some friends of mine on the way, the Fevershams; but I don't believe they're back from Brighton.' That's what he said. What Artemis heard, saw and blasted with her blazing eye, was a typical insolent, selfish, self-indulgent male brazenly bragging in the open street of his intention to go to his infamous club, where women are slandered and men drugged with alcohol. After the shock of this shameless avowal, of course she could not stoop to pick up the pieces of any other silly things he had said. He was simply the man who went to the club.

"Now all those three real statements of Gahagan are exactly the same. They all mean the same thing; map out the same course of action; give the same reasons for the same acts. But they sound totally different according to which sentence comes first; especially to these rather jumpy modern girls, accustomed only to jump at the sentence that comes first—very often because there isn't anything at all to come after it. The Asa-Smith school of drama, in which every sentence stops as soon as it starts, if it doesn't strike you as having much to do with the Tragedy of Cato, has had a very great deal to do with the Tragedy of Captain Gahagan. They might have hanged my friend between them, with the best intentions in the world, simply and solely because they will think only in half-sentences. Broken necks, broken hearts, broken lives, and all because they won't learn any language but broken English. Don't you think there's something to be said for that musty old taste of his and mine, for the sort of literature that makes you read all that a man writes and listen to all that he says? Wouldn't you rather have an important statement made to you in the language of Addison or Johnson than in the splutterings of Mr. Toxin and the Diving Duchess?"

During this monologue, certainly rather long, the lawyer had grown more and more restless and full of nervous irritation.

"This is all fancywork," he said almost feverishly. "You haven't proved any of this."

"No," said Pond gravely, "as you say, I fancied it. At least I guessed it. But I did ring up Gahagan and hear something of the truth of his words and movements that afternoon."

"Truth!" cried Luke, with very extraordinary bitterness.

Pond looked at him curiously. That woodenness of visage which was the first impression produced by Mr. Luke was found on examination to consist mostly of a rather forced look of fixity, combined with the rigid smoothness of his head and hair, the latter looking as if it had been painted on with some rather sticky yellow paint: a gummy gamboge. His eyelids indeed were cold and often partially closed; but inside them the grey-green eyes seemed strangely small, as if they were distant; and they were dancing and darting about like microscopic green flies. The more Mr. Pond looked at those veiled but restless eyes, the less he liked them. The old fancy came back to him about an actual conspiracy against Gahagan; though certainly not one worked by Artemis or Joan. At last he broke the silence very abruptly.

"Mr. Luke," he said, "you are naturally concerned for your late client; but some might feel you had a more than professional interest. Since you study his interests so deeply, can you give me a piece of information about him? *Did* Mr. Feversham and his wife come back from Brighton that day? Was Mrs. Feversham at the house that afternoon, whether Gahagan went there, or not?"

"She was not," said Luke shortly. "They were both expected to return next morning. I have no idea why Feversham himself did return that night."

"Looks almost as if somebody had sent for him," said Mr. Pond.

Mr. Luke the solicitor rose abruptly from his seat and turned away. "I cannot see any use in all these speculations of yours," he said, and, making a stiff salute, he took his top-hat and was gone from the house with a swiftness that seemed hardly normal.

Next day Mr. Pond clad himself even more conventionally and carefully than usual, and proceeded to pay a round of calls on a series of ladies: a frivolous solemnity which with him was by no means usual. The first lady he waited upon was the Hon. Violet Varney, whom he had hitherto only seen in the distance, and was gently depressed at having to see so close. She was what he believed, in these latter days, to be described as a platinum blonde. It was doubtless a graceful reminiscence of her own name which led her to tint her mouth and cheeks with a colour that was rather violet than purple, giving an effect which her friends called ghostly and her foes ghastly. Even from this listless lady he did extract some admissions tending to help in the reconstruction of Gahagan's real remarks; though the lady's own remarks had their usual air of expiring with a gasp before they were really finished. Then he had another interview with her sister, Joan, and marvelled inwardly at the strange thing which is human personality and stands apart from modes and manners. For

Joan had very much the same tricks of style; the same rather high, well-bred voice, the same sketchy, uncompleted sentences; but, fortunately, not the same purple powder and not in the least the same eyes or gestures or mind or immortal soul. Mr. Pond, with all his old-fashioned prejudices, knew at once that in this other girl the new virtues were virtues, whether or not they were new. She really was brave and generous and fond of the truth, though the Society papers did say so. "She's all right," said Mr. Pond to himself. "She's as good as gold. A great deal better than gold. And oh, how much better than platinum!"

Stopping at the next stage of his pilgrimage, he visited the monstrous and ludicrous large hotel which had the honour of housing Miss Artemis Asa-Smith of Pennsylvania. She received him with the rather overwhelming enthusiasm which bore her everywhere through the world; and Mr. Pond had very little difficulty in her case in extracting an admission that even a man who goes to a club may happen not to be a murderer. Though this explanation was naturally less personal and intimate than his interview with Joan (about which he always refused to say a word to anybody), the ardent Artemis continued to earn his approval by her reserves of good sense and good nature. She saw the point about the order of the topics mentioned, and its probable effect on her own mind; and so far the diplomacy of Mr. Pond had been successful. All the three ladies, with whatever degrees of seriousness or concentration, had listened to his theory of what Gahagan had said; and had all agreed that he might very probably have said it. This part of his task being done, Mr. Pond paused a little, and perhaps rather pulled himself together, before approaching his last duty—which also took the form of calling on a lady. He might be excused; for it also involved passing through that grim garden where a man had lain murdered, to that high and sinister house where his widow was still living alone: the great Olivia, queen of tragedy, now tragic by a double claim.

He stepped, not without repugnance, across that dark corner inside the gate and under the holly tree where poor Fred Feversham had been spiked to the earth by a mere splinter of a sword; and as he climbed the crooked path to the doorway in the narrow and bare brick house that stood above him like a tower, dark against the stars, he revolved difficulties much deeper than had yet troubled him in the more trifling matter of the supposed inconsistencies of Gahagan's conversation. There was a real question behind all that nonsense; and it demanded an answer. Somebody had murdered the unfortunate Frederick Feversham; and there were some real reasons for directing the suspicion upon Gahagan. After all, he had been in the habit of spending whole days, or half of the nights as well, with this actress; nothing seemed more horribly natural, more repulsively probable, than that they had been surprised by Feversham and had taken the bloody way out. Mrs. Feversham had often been compared to Mrs. Siddons. Her own external behaviour had always been full of dignity and discretion. A scandal for her was not an advertisement, as it would be for Violet Varney. She had really the stronger motive of the two . . . but, good God, this would never do! Suppose Gahagan really was innocent—but at that price! Whatever his weaknesses, he was just the man to be hanged like a gentleman rather than let The Lady—— He looked up with growing terror at the tower of dark brick, wondering if he were to meet the murderess. . . . Then he furiously flung off the morbidity, and tried again to fix himself on the facts. After all, what was there against Gahagan or the widow? It seemed to him, as he forced himself to colder considerations, that it really resolved itself into a matter of time.

Gahagan had certainly spent a huge amount of *time* with Olivia; that was really the only external proof of his passion for her. The proofs of his passion for Joan were very external indeed. Pond could have sworn that the Irishman was really in love with Joan. He threw himself at her head; and she, on the accepted standards of modern youth, threw herself back at him. But these encounters, one might say collisions, were as brief as they were brilliant. Why did a lover full of such triumphs want to go off and spend such a lot of *time* with a much older woman? . . . These broodings had turned him into an automaton and brought him unconsciously past the servants and up the stairs and into the very room where he was asked to wait for Mrs. Feversham. He nervously picked up an old battered book, apparently dating from the time when the actress was a schoolgirl, for the flyleaf showed in a very schoolgirl hand: "Olivia Malone." Perhaps the great Shakespearian actress claimed descent from the great Shakespearian critic. But, anyhow, she must be Irish—at least by tradition. . . .

As he bent over the shabby book in the dusky anteroom, there shot into his mind a white ray of serene and complete understanding: so far as this tale goes, the last of the paradoxes of Mr. Pond. He felt full and complete certainty; and yet the only words to express it wrote themselves rapidly across his brain with the bewildering brevity of a hieroglyphic.

"Love never needs time. But Friendship always needs time. More and more and more time, up to long past midnight."

When Gahagan had done those crazy things that blazoned his

devotion to Joan Varney, they had hardly occupied any time. When he fell on her from a parachute as she came out of church at Bournemouth, the fall was naturally very rapid. When he tore up a return ticket costing hundreds of pounds to stay with her half an hour longer in Samoa, it was only half an hour longer. When he swam the Hellespont in imitation of Leander, it was only for exactly thirty-five minutes' conversation with Hero. But Love is like that. It is a thing of great moments; and it lives on the memory of moments. Perhaps it is a fragile illusion; perhaps, on the other hand, it is eternal and beyond time. But Friendship eats up time. If poor Gahagan had a real intellectual friendship, then he would go on talking till long past midnight. And with whom would Gahagan be so likely to have one as with an Irish actress who was chiefly interested in Shakespeare? Even as he had the thought, he heard the rich and faintly Irish voice of Olivia welcoming him; and he knew he was right.

"Don't you know," asked the widow with a mournful smile, when he had tactfully steered the conversation past condolences to Captain Gahagan, "don't you know we poor Irishes have a secret vice? It's called Poetry; or perhaps I ought to say it's generally called Recitation. It's been suppressed by the police in all the English salons; and that's the worst of the Irish wrongs. People in London are not allowed to recite poems to each other all night, as they do in Dublin. Poor Peter used to come to me and talk Shakespeare till morning; but I had to turn him out at last. When a man calls on *me*, and tries to recite the whole of *Romeo and Juliet*, it gets past a joke. But you see how it was. The English won't allow the poor fellow to recite Shakespeare."

Mr. Pond did indeed see how it was. He knew enough about men to know that a man must have a friend, if possible a female friend, to talk to till all is blue. He knew enough about Dubliners to know that neither devils nor dynamite will stop them from reciting verse. All the black clouds of morbid brooding on the murder which had oppressed him in the garden had rolled away at the first sound of this strong, good-humoured Irishwoman's voice. But after a little while they began to gather again, though more remotely. After all, as he had said before, *somebody* had killed poor Fred Feversham.

He was quite certain now that it was not Feversham's wife. He was practically certain it was not Gahagan. He went home that night turning the question over and over; but he had only one night's unrest. For the next day's paper contained the news of the unexplained suicide of Mr. Luke, of the well-known firm of Masters, Luke and Masters; and Mr. Pond sat gently chiding himself, because he had not thought of the obvious fact that a man who is always tearing and rending people because he has been swindled, may possibly discover one day that he has been swindled by his own solicitor. Feversham had summoned Luke to that midnight meeting in the garden, in order to tell him so; but Mr. Luke, a man careful of his professional standing, had taken very prompt steps to prevent Mr. Feversham telling anybody else.

"It makes me feel very bad," said Mr. Pond, meekly and almost tremulously. "At that last meeting of ours I could see he was awfully frightened already; and, do you know, I'm very much afraid that it was I who frightened him."

WHEN DOCTORS AGREE

M<small>R. POND'S</small> paradoxes were of a very peculiar kind. They were indeed paradoxical defiances even of the law of paradox. Paradox has been defined as "Truth standing on her head to attract attention." Paradox has been defended; on the ground that so many fashionable fallacies still stand firmly on their feet, because they have no heads to stand on. But it must be admitted that writers, like other mendicants and mountebanks, frequently do try to attract attention. They set out conspicuously, in a single line in a play, or at the head or tail of a paragraph, remarks of this challenging kind; as when Mr. Bernard Shaw wrote: "The Golden Rule is that there is no Golden Rule"; or Oscar Wilde observed: "I can resist everything except temptation"; or a duller scribe (not to be named with these and now doing penance for his earlier vices in the nobler toil of celebrating the virtues of Mr. Pond) said in defence of hobbies and amateurs and general duffers like himself: "If a thing is worth doing, it is worth doing badly." To these things do writers sink; and then the critics tell them that they "talk for effect"; and then the writers answer: "What the devil else should we talk for? Ineffectualness?" It is a sordid scene.

But Mr. Pond belonged to a more polite world and his paradoxes were quite different. It was quite impossible to imagine Mr. Pond standing on his head. But it was quite as easy to imagine him standing on his head as to imagine him trying to attract attention. He was the quietest man in the world to be a man of the world; he was a small, neat Civil Servant; with nothing notable about him except a beard that looked not only old-fashioned but vaguely foreign, and perhaps a little French, though he was as English as any man alive. But, for that matter, French respectability is far more respectable than English; and Mr. Pond, though in some ways cosmopolitan, was completely respectable. Another thing that was faintly French about him was the level ripple of his speech: a tripping monotone that never tripped over a single vowel. For the French carry their sense of equality even to the equality of syllables. With this equable flow, full of genteel gossip on Vienna, he was once entertaining a lady; and five minutes later she rejoined her friends with a very white face; and whispered to them the shocking secret that the mild little man was mad.

The peculiarity of his conversation was this: in the middle of a steady stream of sense, there would suddenly appear two or three words which seemed simply to be nonsense. It was as if something had suddenly gone wrong with the works of a gramophone. It was nonsense which the speaker never seemed to notice himself; so that sometimes his hearers also hardly noticed that speech so natural was nonsensical. But to those who did notice, he seemed to be saying something like, "Naturally, having no legs, he won the walking-race easily," or "As there was nothing to drink, they all got tipsy at once." Broadly speaking, two kinds of people stopped him with stares or questions: the very stupid and the very clever. The stupid because the absurdity alone stuck out from a level of intelligence that baffled them; it was indeed in itself an example of the truth in paradox. The only part of his conversation they could understand was the part they could not understand. And the clever stopped him because they knew that, behind each of these queer compact contradictions, there was a very queer story—like the queer story to be narrated here.

His friend Gahagan, that ginger-haired giant and somewhat flippant Irish dandy, declared that Pond put in these senseless phrases merely to find out whether his listeners were listening. Pond never said so; and his motive remained rather a mystery. But Gahagan declared that there is a whole tribe of modern intellectual ladies, who have learned nothing except the art of turning on a talker a face of ardour and attention, while their minds are so very absent that some little phrase like, "Finding himself in India, he naturally visited Toronto," will pass harmlessly in at one ear and out at the other, without disturbing the cultured mind within.

It was at a little dinner given by old Wotton to Gahagan and Pond and others, that we first got a glimpse of the real meaning of these wild parentheses of so tame a talker. The truth was, to begin with, that Mr. Pond, in spite of his French beard, was very English in his habit of assuming that he ought to be a little dull, in deference to other people. He disliked telling long and largely fantastic stories about himself, such as his friend Gahagan told, though Pond thoroughly enjoyed them when Gahagan told them. Pond himself had had some very curious experiences; but, as he would not turn them into long stories, they appeared only as short stories; and the short stories were so very short as to be quite unintelligible. In trying to explain the eccentricity, it is best to begin with the simplest example, like a diagram in a primer of logic. And I will begin with the short story, which was concealed in the shorter phrase, which puzzled poor old Wotton so completely on that particular evening. Wotton was an old-fashioned diplomatist, of the sort that seemed to grow more national by trying to be international. Though far from militarist, he was very military. He kept the peace by staccato sentences under a stiff grey moustache. He had more chin than forehead.

"They tell me," Wotton was saying, "that the Poles and Lithuanians have come to an agreement about Wilno. It was an old row, of course; and I expect it was six to one and half a dozen to the other."

"You are a real Englishman, Wotton," said Gahagan, "and you say in your heart, 'All these foreigners are alike.' You're right enough if you mean that we're all unlike you. The English are the lunatics of the earth, who know that everybody else is mad. But we do sometimes differ a little from each other, you know. Even we in Ireland have been known to differ from each other. But you see the Pope denouncing the Bolshevists, or the French Revolution rending the Holy Roman Empire, and you still say in your hearts, 'What can the difference be betwixt Tweedledum and Tweedledee?' "

"There was no difference," said Pond, "between Tweedledum and Tweedledee. You will remember that it is distinctly recorded that they agreed. But remember what they agreed about."

Wotton looked a little baffled and finally grunted: "Well, if these fellows have agreed, I suppose there will be a little peace."

"Funny things, agreements," said Pond. "Fortunately people generally go on disagreeing, till they die peacefully in their beds. Men very seldom do fully and finally agree. I did know two men who came to agree so completely that one of them naturally murdered the other; but as a rule . . ."

" 'Agreed so completely,' " said Wotton thoughtfully. "Don't you—are you quite sure you don't mean: 'Disagreed so completely'?"

Gahagan uttered a sort of low whoop of laughter. "Oh, no," he said, "he doesn't mean that. I don't know what the devil he does mean; but he doesn't mean anything so sensible as that."

But Wotton, in his ponderous way, still attempted to pin down the narrator to a more responsible statement; and the upshot of it was that Mr. Pond was reluctantly induced to explain what he really meant and let us hear the whole story.

The mystery was involved at first in another mystery: the strange murder of Mr. James Haggis, of Glasgow, which filled the Scottish and English newspapers not many years ago. On the face of it, the thing was a curious story; to introduce a yet more curious sequel. Haggis had been a prominent and wealthy citizen, a bailie of the city and an elder of the kirk. Nobody denied that even in these capacities he had sometimes been rather unpopular; but, to do him justice, he had often been unpopular through his loyalty to unpopular causes. He was the sort of old Radical who is more rigid and antiquated than any Tory; and, maintaining in theory the cause of Retrenchment and Reform, he managed to suggest that almost any Reform was too expensive for the needs of Retrenchment. Thus he had stood alone in opposition to the universal support given to old Dr. Campbell's admirable campaign for fighting the epidemic in the slums during the slump. But to deduce from his economics that he was a demon delighting in the sight of poor children dying of typhoid was perhaps an exaggerated inference. Similarly, he was prominent in the Presbyterian councils as refusing all modern compromise with the logic of Calvinism; but to infer that he actually hoped all his neighbours were damned before they were born is too personal an interpretation of theological theory.

On the other side, he was admittedly honest in business and faithful to his wife and family; so that there was a general reaction in favour of his memory when he was found stabbed to the heart in the meagre grass of the grim little churchyard that adjoined his favourite place of worship. It was impossible to imagine Mr. Haggis as involved in any romantic Highland feud calling for the dirk, or any romantic assignation interrupted with the stiletto; and it was generally felt that to be knifed and left unburied among the buried dead was an exaggerated penalty for being a rather narrow Scottish merchant of the old school.

It happened that Mr. Pond himself had been present at a little party where there was high debate about the murder as a mystery. His host,

Lord Glenorchy, had a hobby of reading books on criminology; his hostess, Lady Glenorchy, had the less harmful hobby of reading those much more solid and scientific books which are called detective stories. There were present, as the society papers say, Major MacNabb, the Chief Constable, and Mr. Launcelot Browne, a brilliant London barrister who found it much more of a bore to be a lawyer than to pretend to be a detective; also, among those present, was the venerable and venerated Dr. Campbell, whose work among the poor has already been inadequately commended, and a young friend of his named Angus, whom he was understood to be coaching and instructing generally for his medical examinations and his scientific career.

Responsible people naturally love to be irresponsible. All these persons delighted to throw theories about in private which they need not answer for in public. The barrister, being a humane man, was delighted to prosecute somebody whom he would not have to hang. The criminologist was enchanted to analyse the lunacy of somebody he could never have proved to be a lunatic. And Lady Glenorchy was charmed at the chance of considering poor Mr. Haggis (of all people) as the principal character in a shocker. Hilarious attempts were made to fix the crime on the United Presbyterian minister, a notorious Sublapsarian, naturally, nay inevitably, impelled to stick a dirk in a Supralapsarian. Lord Glenorchy was more serious, not to say monotonous. Having learnt from his books of criminology the one great discovery of that science, that mental and moral deformity are found only among poor people, he suspected a plot of local Communists (all with the wrong-shaped thumb and ear) and picked for his fancy a Socialist agitator of the city. Mr. Angus made bold to differ; his choice was an old lag, or professional criminal, known to be in the place, who had been almost everything that is alarming except a Socialist agitator. Then it was that the point was referred, not without a certain reverence, to the white-haired and wise old physician, who had now behind him a whole lifetime of charity and good works. One of the many ways in which Dr. Campbell seemed to have emerged from an elder and perhaps honester world was the fact that he not only spoke with a Scottish accent but he spoke Scottish. His speech will, therefore, be rendered here with difficulty and in doubt and trembling.

"Weel, ye will a' be asking wha dirked Jamie Haggis? And I'll tell ye fair at the start that I winna gie a bawbee to ken wha dirked Jamie Haggis. Gin I kent, I wadna' say. It's a sair thing, na doot, that the freens and benefactors o' puir humanity should no be named and fitly celebrated; but like the masons that built our gran' cathedral and the gran' poets that wrote our ballads of Otterburn and Sir Patrick Spens, the man that achieved the virtuous act o' killing Jamie Haggis will ha'e nae pairsonal credit for't in this world; it is even possible he might be a wee bit inconvenienced. So ye'll get nae guesses out of me; beyond saying I've lang been seekin' a man of sic prudence and public spirit."

There followed that sort of silence in which people are not certain whether to laugh, at a deliberate stroke of wit; but before they could do so, young Angus, who kept his eyes fixed on his venerable preceptor, had spoken with the eagerness of the ardent student.

"But you'll not say, Dr. Campbell, that murder is right because some acts or opinions of the murdered man are wrong?"

"Aye, if they're wrang enough," replied the benevolent Dr. Campbell blandly. "After all, we've nae ither test o' richt and wrang. *Salus populi suprema lex.*"

"Aren't the Ten Commandments a bit of a test?" asked the young man, with a rather heated countenance, emphasized by his red hair, that stood up on his head like stiff flames.

The silver-haired saint of sociology continued to regard him with a wholly benevolent smile; but there was an odd gleam in his eye as he answered:

"Aye, the Ten Commandments are a test. What we doctors are beginning to ca' an Intelligence Test."

Whether it was an accident, or whether the intuitions of Lady Glenorchy were a little alarmed by the seriousness of the subject, it was at this point that she struck in.

"Well, if Dr. Campbell won't pronounce for us, I suppose we must all stick to our own suspicions. I don't know whether you like cigarettes in the middle of dinner; it's a fashion I can't get used to myself."

At this point in his narrative, Mr. Pond threw himself back in his chair with a more impatient movement than he commonly permitted himself.

"Of course, they will do it," he said, with a mild explosiveness. "They're admired and thought very tactful when they do it."

"When who do what?" said Wotton. "What on earth are you talking about now?"

"I'm talking about hostesses," said Pond, with an air of pain. "Good hostesses. Really successful hostesses. They will cut into conversation, on the theory that it can be broken off anywhere. Just as it's quite the definition of a good hostess to make two people talk when they hate it, and part them when they are beginning to like it. But they sometimes do the most deadly and awful damage. You see, they stop conversations that are not worth starting again. And that's horrible, like murder."

"But if the conversation's not worth starting again, why is it horrible to stop it?" asked the conscientious Wotton, still laboriously in pursuit.

"Why, *that's* why it's horrible to stop it," answered Pond, almost snappishly for so polite a person. "Talk ought to be sacred because it is so light, so tenuous, so trivial, if you will; anyhow, so frail and easy to destroy. Cutting short its life is worse than murder; it's infanticide. It's like killing a baby that's trying to come to life. It can never be restored to life, though one rose from the dead. A good light conversation can never be put together again when it's broken to pieces; because you can't get all the pieces. I remember a splendid talk at Trefusis's place, that began because there was a crack of thunder over the house and a cat howled in the garden, and somebody made a rather crude joke about a catastrophe. And then Gahagan here had a perfectly lovely theory that sprang straight out of cats and catastrophes and everything, and would have started a splendid talk about a political question on the Continent."

"The Catalonian question, I suppose," said Gahagan, laughing, "but I fear I've quite forgotten my lovely theory."

"That's just what I say," said Pond, gloomily. "It could only have been started then; it ought to have been sacred because it wasn't worth starting again. The hostess swept it all out of our heads, and then had the cheek to say afterwards that we could talk about it some other time. Could we? Could we make a contract with a cloud to break just over the roof, and tie a cat up in the garden and pull its tail at the right moment, and give Gahagan just enough champagne to inspire him with a theory so silly that he's forgotten it already? It was then or never with that debate being started; and yet bad results enough followed from it being stopped. But that, as they say, is another story."

"You must tell it to us another time," said Gahagan. "At present I am still curious about the man who murdered another man because he agreed with him."

"Yes," assented Wotton, "we've rather strayed from the subject, haven't we?"

"So Mrs. Trefusis said," murmured Mr. Pond sadly. "I suppose we can't all feel the sanctity of really futile conversation. But if you're really interested in the other matter, I don't mind telling you all about it; though I'd rather not tell you exactly how I came to know all about it. That was rather a confidential matter—what they call a confession. Pardon my little interlude on the tactful hostess; it had something to do with what followed and I have a reason for mentioning it.

"Lady Glenorchy quite calmly changed the subject from murder to cigarettes; and everybody's first feeling was that we had been done out of a very entertaining little tiff about the Ten Commandments. A mere trifle, too light and airy to recur to our minds at any other time. But there was another trifle that did recur to my own mind afterwards; and kept my attention on a murder of which I might have thought little enough at the time, as De Quincey says. I remembered once looking up Glenorchy in *Who's Who*, and seeing that he had married the daughter of a very wealthy squire near Lowestoft in Suffolk."

"Lowestoft, Suffolk. These are dark hints," said Gahagan. "Do these in themselves point to some awful and suspicious fact?"

"They point," said Pond, "to the awful fact that Lady Glenorchy is not Scottish. If she had introduced the cigarettes at her father's dinner-table in Suffolk, such trifles as the Ten Commandments would instantly have been tossed away from everyone's mind and memory. But I knew I was in Scotland and that the story had only just begun. I have told you that old Campbell was tutoring or coaching young Angus for his medical degree. It was a great honour for a lad like Angus to have Campbell for a coach; but it must have been quite agreeable even to an authority like Campbell to have Angus for a pupil. For he had always been a most industrious and ambitious and intelligent pupil, and one likely to do the old man credit; and after the time I speak of, he seemed to grow more industrious and ambitious than ever. In fact, he shut himself up so exclusively with his coach that he failed in his examination. That was what first convinced me that my guess was right."

"And very lucid, too," said Gahagan with a grin. "He worked so hard with his coach that he failed in his examination. Another statement that might seem to some to require expansion."

"It's very simple, really," said Mr. Pond innocently. "But in order to expand it, we must go back for a moment to the mystery of Mr. Haggis's murder. It had already spread a sort of detective fever in the neighbourhood; for all the Scots love arguing and it really was rather a fascinating riddle. One great point in the mystery was the wound, which seemed at first to have been made by a dirk or dagger of some kind but was afterwards found by the experts to demand a different instrument of rather peculiar shape. Moreover, the district had been combed for knives and daggers; and temporary suspicion fixed on any wild youths from beyond the Highland line, who might retain an historic tenderness for the possession of dirks. All the medical authorities agreed that the instrument had been something more subtle than a dirk, though no medical authorities would consent even to guess what it was. People were perpetually ransacking the churchyard and the church in search of clues. And just about this time young Angus, who had been a strict supporter of this particular church, and had even once induced his old tutor and friend to sit under its minister for one evening service, suddenly left off going there; indeed, he left off going to any church at all. So I realized that I was still on the right track."

"Oh," said Wotton blankly, "so you realized that you were still on the right track."

"I fear I did not realize that you were on any track," said Gahagan. "To speak with candour, my dear Pond, I should say that of all the trackless and aimless and rambling human statements I have ever heard, the most rambling was the narrative we have just been privileged to hear from you. First you tell us that two Scotsmen began a conversation about the morality of murder and never finished it; then you go off on a tirade against society hostesses; then you reveal the horrid fact that one of them came from Lowestoft; then you go back to one of the Scotsmen and say he failed to pass his examination because he worked so hard with his tutor; then, pausing for a moment upon the peculiar shape of an undiscovered dagger, you tell us that the Scotsman has left off going to church and you are on the right track. Frankly, if you really do find something sacred about futile conversation, I should say that you were on the track of that all right."

"I know," said Mr. Pond patiently, "all I've said is quite relevant to what really happened; but, of course, you don't know what really happened. A story always does seem rambling and futile if you leave out what really happened. That's why newspapers are so dull. All the political news, and much of the police news (though rather higher in tone than the other), is made quite bewildering and pointless by the necessity of telling stories without telling the story."

"Well, then," said Gahagan, "let us try to get some sense out of all this nonsense, which has not even the excuses of newspaper nonsense. To take one of your nonsense remarks as a test, why do you say that Angus failed to pass because he worked so much with his coach?"

"Because he didn't work with his coach," replied Pond. "Because I didn't say he worked with his coach. At least I didn't say he worked for the examination. I said he was with his coach. I said he spent days and nights with his coach; but they weren't preparing for any examination."

"Well, what were they doing?" asked Wotton gruffly.

"They were going on with the argument," cried Pond, in a squeak that was almost shrill. "They hardly stopped to sleep or eat; but they went on with the argument; the argument interrupted at the dinner-table. Have you never known any Scotsmen? Do you suppose that a woman from Suffolk with a handful of cigarettes, and a mouthful of irrelevance, can stop two Scotsmen from going on with an argument when they've started it? They began it again when they were getting their hats and coats; they were at it hammer and tongs as they went out of the gate, and only a Scottish poet can describe what they did then:

> And the tane went hame with the ither; and then,
> The tither went hame with the ither again.

"And for hours and weeks and months they never turned aside from the same interminable debate on the thesis first propounded by Dr. Campbell: that when a good man is well and truly convinced that a bad man is actively bad for the community, and is doing evil on a large scale which cannot be checked by law or any other action, the good man has a moral right to murder the bad man, and thereby only increases his own goodness."

Pond paused a moment, pulling his beard and staring at the table; then he began again:

"For reasons I've already mentioned but not explained——"

"That's what's the matter with you, my boy," said Gahagan genially. "There are always such a damned lot of things you have mentioned but not explained."

"For those reasons," went on Pond deliberately, "I happen to know a great deal about the stages of that stubborn and forcible controversy, about which nobody else knew anything at all. For Angus was a genuine truth-seeker who wished to satisfy his soul and not merely to make his name; and Campbell was enough of a great man to be quite as anxious to convince a pupil as to convince a crowd in a lecture-room. But I am not going to tell you about those stages of the controversy at any great length. To tell the truth, I am not what people call impartial on this controversy. How any man can form any conviction, and remain what they call impartial on any controversy, is more than I have ever understood. But I suppose they would say I couldn't describe the debate fairly; because the side I sympathize with was not the side that won.

"Society hostesses, especially when they come from near Lowestoft, do not know where an argument is tending. They will drop not only bricks but bombshells; and then expect them not to explode. Anyhow, I knew where that argument at Glenorchy's table was tending. When Angus made a test of the Ten Commandments, and Campbell said they were an Intelligence Test, I knew what would come next. In another minute, he would be saying that nobody of intelligence now troubles about the Ten Commandments.

"What a disguise there is in snowy hair and the paternal stoop of age! Dickens somewhere describes a patriarch who needed no virtue except his white hair. As Dr. Campbell smiled across the table at Angus, most people saw nothing in that smile but patriarchal and parental kindness. But I happened to see also a glint in the eye, which told me that the old man was quite as much of a fighter as the red-haired boy who had rashly challenged him. In some odd way, indeed, I seemed suddenly to see old age itself as a masquerade. The white hair had turned into a white wig, the powder of the eighteenth century; and the smiling face underneath it was the face of Voltaire.

"Dr. Andrew Glenlyon Campbell was a real philanthropist; so was Voltaire. It is not always certain whether philanthropy means a love of men, or of man, or of mankind. There is a difference. I think he cared less about the individual than about the public or the race; hence doubtless his gentle eccentricity of defending an act of private execution. But anyhow, I knew he was one of the grim line of Scottish sceptics, from Hume down to Ross or Robertson. And, whatever else they are, they are stubborn and stick to their point. Angus also was stubborn, and as I have already said, he was a devout worshipper in the same dingy kirk as the late James Haggis; that is, one of the extreme irreconcilable sectaries of the seventeenth-century Puritanism. And so the Scottish atheist and the Scottish Calvinist argued and argued and argued, until milder races might have expected them to drop down dead with fatigue. But it was not of disagreement that either of them died.

"But the advantage was with the older and more learned man in his attack; and you must remember that the younger man had only a rather narrow and provincial version of the creed to defend. As I say, I will not bore you with the arguments; I confess they rather bore me. Doubtless Dr. Campbell said that the Ten Commandments could not be of divine origin, because two of them are mentioned by the virtuous Emperor Foo Chi, in the Second Dynasty; or one of them is paraphrased by Synesius of Samothrace and attributed to the lost code of Lycurgus."

"Who was Synesius of Samothrace?" inquired Gahagan, with an appearance of sudden and eager curiosity.

"He was a mythical character of the Minoan Age first discovered in the twentieth century A.D.," replied the unruffled Pond. "I made him up just now; but you know the sort of thing I mean—the mythical nature of Mount Sinai proved from the parallel myth that the ark rested on Mount Ararat, and the mountain that would not come to Mahomet. But all this textual criticism really affects a religion only founded on texts. I knew how the fight was going; and I knew when it ended. I knew when Robert Angus left off going to kirk on the Sabbath."

The end of the debate may best be described more directly; for, indeed, Mr. Pond described it himself with a strange sort of directness; almost as if he had unaccountably been present, or had seen it in a vision. Anyhow, it appears that the operating-theatre of the medical schools was the scene of the final phase of disagreement and agreement. They had gone back there very late at night, when the schools were closed and the theatre deserted, because Angus fancied he had left some of his instruments there, which it would be more neat and proper to lock up. There was no sound in that hollow place but the echo of their own footsteps, and very little light save a faint moonshine that trickled through the cracks between the curtained windows. Angus had retrieved his operating-tool, and was turning again towards the steep stairs that climbed through the semi-circular rows of seats, when Campbell said to him casually:

"Ye'll find the facts I mentioned aboot the Aztec hymns in the——"

Angus tossed the tool on the table like a man throwing down his sword, and turned on his companion with a new and transfigured air of candour and finality.

"You needn't trouble about hymns any more; I may as well tell you that I've done with them, for one. You're too strong for me—or, rather, the truth is too strong for me. I've defended my own nursery nightmare as long as I could; but you've woken me up at last. You are right, you must be right; I don't see any way out of it."

After a silence, Campbell answered very softly: "I'll no mak' apologies for fighting for the truth; but, man, ye made a real bonny fight for the falsehood."

It might well have seemed that the old blasphemer had never spoken on the topic in a tone so delicate and respectful; and it seemed strange that his new convert did not respond to the appeal. Looking up, Campbell saw that his new convert's attention had been abruptly abstracted; he was standing staring at the implement in his hand: a surgical knife made upon an odd pattern for special purposes. At last he said in a hoarse and almost inaudible voice:

"A knife of an unusual shape."

"See report o' inquest on Jamie Haggis," said the old man, nodding benevolently. "Aye, ye've guessed richt, I'm thinking." Then, after a pause, he added, with equal calm:

"Noo that we are agreed, and a' of one mind, aboot the need for sic social surgery, it's as weel ye should know the hale truth. Aye, lad, I did it mysel'; and with a blade like yon. That nicht ye took me to the kirk—weel, it's the fairst time, I hope, I've ever been hypocreetical; but I stayed behind to pray, and I think ye had hopes of my convairsion. But I prayed because Jamie prayed; and when he rose from his prayers, I followed him and killed him i' the kirkyard."

Angus was still looking at the knife in silence; then he said suddenly: "Why did you kill him?"

"Ye needna ask, noo we are agreed in moral philosophy," replied the old doctor simply. "It was just plain surgery. As we sacrifice a finger to save the body, so we maun sacrifice a man to save the body politic. I killed him because he was doing evil, and inhumanly preventing what was guid for humanity: the scheme for the slums and the lave. And I understand that, upon reflection, ye tak the same view."

Angus nodded grimly.

The proverb asks: "Who shall decide when doctors disagree?" But in that dark and ominous theatre of doctoring the doctors agreed.

"Yes," said Angus, "I take the same view. Also, I have had the same experience."

"And what's that?" inquired the other.

"I have had daily dealings with a man I thought was doing nothing but evil," answered Angus. "I still think you were doing evil; even though you were serving truth. You have convinced me that my beliefs were dreams; but not that dreaming is worse than waking up. You brutally broke the dreams of the humble, sneered at the weak hopes of the bereaved. You seem cruel and inhuman to me, just as Haggis seemed cruel and inhuman to you. You are a good man by your own code, but so was Haggis a good man by his code. He did not pretend to believe in salvation by good works, any more than you pretended to believe in the Ten Commandments. He was good to individuals, but the crowd suffered; you are good to the crowd and an individual suffered. But, after all, you also are only an individual."

Something in the last words, that were said very softly, made the old doctor stiffen suddenly and then start backwards towards the steps behind. Angus sprang like a wildcat and pinned him to his place with a choking violence; still talking, but now at the top of his voice.

"Day after day, I have itched and tingled to kill you; and been held back only by the superstition you have destroyed to-night. Day after day, you have been battering down the scruples which alone defended you from death. You wise thinker; you wary reasoner; you fool! It would be better for you to-night if I still believed in God and in his Commandment against murder."

The old man twisted speechlessly in the throttling grip, but he was too feeble, and Angus flung him with a crash across the operating-table, where he lay as if fainting. Round them and above them the empty tiers of concentric seats glimmered in the faint and frigid moonlight as desolate as the Colosseum under the moon; a deserted amphitheatre where there was no human voice to cry *"Habet!"* The red-haired slayer stood with the knife uplifted, as strange in shape as the flint knife of some prehistoric sacrifice; and still he talked on in the high tones of madness.

"One thing alone protected you and kept the peace between us: that we disagreed. Now we agree, now we are at one in thought—and deed, I can do as you would do. I can do as you have done. We are at peace."

And with the sound of that word he struck; and Andrew Campbell moved for the last time. In his own cold temple, upon his own godless altar . . . he stirred and then lay still; and the murderer bent and fled from the building and from the city and across the Highland line at night, to hide himself in the hills.

When Pond had told this story, Gahagan rose slowly to his gigantic height and knocked out his cigar in an ashtray: "I darkly suspect, Pond," he said, "that you are not quite so irrelevant as you sound. Not quite irrelevant, I mean, even to our opening talk about European affairs."

"Tweedledum and Tweedledee agreed—to have a battle," said Pond. "We are rather easily satisfied with saying that some people like Poles or Prussians or other foreigners have agreed. We don't often ask what they've agreed on. But agreement can be rather risky, unless it's agreement with the truth."

Wotton looked at him with a smouldering suspicion; but finally decided, with a sigh of relief, that it was only metaphysics.

POND THE PANTALOON

"NO, NO, NO," said Mr. Pond, with a gentle shrillness which he occasionally showed, when any doubt was thrown on the prosaic precision of his statements or arguments. "I did not say it was a red pencil, and that was why it made such black marks. I said it was relatively a red pencil, or resembled a red pencil, as compared with Wotton's view in regarding it as a blue pencil; and *that* was why it made such black marks. The distinction may seem a small one; but I assure you the most enormous errors arise out of this habit of taking a remark out of its context, and then stating it not quite correctly. The most ordinary and obvious truths, when reported in that way, may be made to sound almost absurd."

"Almost," said Captain Gahagan, nodding gravely and gazing at the little man opposite him, rather as if he were a mysterious monster in a tank.

Mr. Pond was in his private tank, or private office, in a hive of Government offices, sitting at a desk and busy at the work of blue-pencilling the proofs of some official report; whence had arisen the talk about the colour of the pencil. Pond, in short, was doing his morning's work as usual; Peter Gahagan was doing nothing, also as usual; his large figure lounged in a chair that looked too small for him; he was attached to Mr. Pond and even more attached to watching other people work.

"I may resemble Polonius," said Pond, modestly; and, indeed, his old-fashioned beard, owlish expression and official courtliness made the comparison almost apt. "I may be like Polonius; but I am not Polonius—which is just the point I wish to illustrate. Hamlet told Polonius that a cloud in the sky was like a camel. The effect would have been somewhat different if Hamlet had stated, seriously and scientifically, that he had seen a camel in the sky. In that case, Polonius might have been pardoned in regarding the Prince's madness as finally proved. Touchy officials have been known to express the view that you, my dear Gahagan, come into this office like a buffalo, and there 'lie wallowing through the long summer day,' as an outmoded poet puts it. But if the authorities of the Zoo sent for you on the ground that you actually *were* a buffalo, the department would hardly move in the matter without further inquiries."

"No doubt you have my *dossier*," said Gahagan, "with official calculations and statistics about the number of my legs, not to mention my horns; all annotated with blue and red pencil—and most certainly with some very black marks against my name. But that brings me back to the original subject of my simple wonder. You hardly seem to have noticed what was really peculiar in your own remark. In any case, I do not quite understand what you mean by a pencil being relatively red. . . ."

"Even that phrase might be defended," observed Mr. Pond, with a faint smile. "You would say, for instance, that my notes on this proof are in blue pencil; and yet——" He held out a pencil with its red chalk point towards the other. It looked like a mild conjuring trick, until he twiddled it so as to show it was one of those pencils sold by most stationers, with red at one end and blue at the other. "Now suppose I wear down the blue point till it has nearly gone (and really the misprints they can put into a simple report on Baluchistan Bi-metallism are incredible), then you would say the pencil was relatively red, though still perhaps rather blue. If the red end were worn away, you would say it was mostly blue, though a little red."

"I should say nothing of the sort," exclaimed Gahagan with abrupt impatience. "I should say what I said before; that the queer thing about you is that you are quite blind to what was really mad in your statement. You can't see the paradox in your own remark. You can't see the point of your own remark."

"The point of my remark," said Mr. Pond, with dignity, "which I thought I had made sufficiently clear, was that people are very inexact in reporting statements, as in cases like a camel and 'something like a camel.' "

Peter Gahagan continued to stare with round eyes at his friend, like a buffalo in a very ruminant phase; and eventually heaved himself up, collecting his grey top-hat and walking-stick with a sort of clatter.

"No," he said, "I will not point out the point. It would be breaking a crystal or shattering a perfectly rounded soap-bubble. To pierce the pure and spherical perfection of your maniacal calm would be like invading the innocence of a child. If you really and truly do not know when you are talking nonsense, if you do not even notice what part of it is nonsense, I feel I must leave your nonsensical intellect intact. I will go and talk it over with Wotton. As he has often breezily observed, there is no nonsense about him."

And he sauntered out of the room, swinging his stick, in the direction of the very important department presided over by Sir Hubert Wotton; that he might enjoy the inspiriting spectacle of another friend doing his day's work and being interrupted by an idle man.

Sir Hubert Wotton, however, was of a type somewhat different from Mr. Pond; in that, even if he was busy, he was never fussy. Mr. Pond was bent over the poised point of his blue pencil; Sir Hubert was first visible behind the red end of a cigar, which he was puffing, with a frown of reflection, as he turned over the papers on his desk. He recognized the entry of the beaming Captain with a grim but not ungracious smile, and waved him to a seat.

Gahagan sat down with his hands crossed on his stick and thumped it on the floor.

"Wotton," he said, "I've solved the problem of the Paradoxes of Pond. He doesn't know when he's said these crazy things. There's a blind spot on his excellent brain, or a cloud comes over his mind for a moment; and he forgets that he's even said anything peculiar. He goes on arguing about the reasonable part of his speech; he never stops to explain the only thing that was really unreasonable. He talked to me quite sensibly about a pencil that was bright red, or something like it, and therefore marked very black on the paper. I tried to nail him to that piece of inconsequence; and he completely eluded me. He went on talking about when a blue pencil was not a blue pencil; but he somehow forgot all about the black marks."

"Black marks!" said Wotton; and sat up so abruptly that he spilt the ash of his cigar over his usually immaculate waistcoat. He dusted off the defilement with a frown; and then, after a pause, spoke in the staccato fashion that occasionally revealed that he was much less conventional than he looked.

"Most fellows who talk paradoxes are only trying to show off. It's not like that with Pond; he does it because he's trying *not* to show off. You see—he looks a very sedentary, scientific little cuss, as if he'd never been unhooked from a desk or a typewriter; but he's really had some very extraordinary experiences. He doesn't talk about them; he doesn't want to talk about them; but he does want to talk about reason and philosophy and theoretical things in books; you know he loves reading all the rational eighteenth-century literature. But when, in the course of talking in the abstract, he comes on some concrete thing that he has actually *done*—well, I can only say he crumples it up. He tries to crush it into a small space and it simply sounds contradictory. Almost every one of those crazy sentences simply stands for one of the adventures in what would be called by most people a very unadventurous life."

"I think I see what you mean," said Gahagan, after a pause of radiant reflection. "Yes, you're right. You can't expect me to be taken in, mind you, by most of your swagger of stoicism in the English public-school man. Half the time they are simply showing off by not showing off. But in Pond it's genuine. He really does hate the limelight; in that way you may say he was made for the Secret Service. And you mean that he only becomes mysterious, in this particular manner, when he really does want to keep the secret of his services. In other words, you mean there is a story behind every paradox of Pond. Certainly that is true—of all those cases when I have been told the story."

"I know all about this story," said Wotton, "and it was one of the most remarkable things that Pond ever did. It was a matter of immense importance—the sort of public affair that has to be kept a very private affair. Pond gave two pieces of advice, which some thought very odd and which turned out exactly right; and he ended by making a rather extraordinary discovery. I don't know how he came to mention it just now; but I'm pretty sure it was by accident. When it turned up, he tried to tuck it away again in a hurry and change the subject. But he certainly saved England; also he nearly got killed."

"What!" exclaimed Gahagan with some astonishment.

"The fellow must have fired five times at him," said Wotton reminiscently, "before he turned the sixth shot on himself."

"Well, I'm blowed," said the Captain elegantly. "I always thought Pond the most charming of tea-table comedies; I never knew he figured in a melodrama. I should as soon have thought of his figuring in a fairy-pantomime. But he seems somehow associated with theatrical things at the moment. He asked me himself if he was like

Polonius; and I suppose some malicious people would say he was more like Pantaloon. I like the notion of you and he magically transplanted to a Christmas pantomime: 'Harlequin Hubert and the Fairies' Pond,' all ending with a real Harlequinade, with red fire and the Pantaloon falling over the Policeman. Pardon my talking nonsense—you know my unfortunate mind only becomes fertile about impossible things."

"It's curious you should call it impossible," said Sir Hubert Wotton, knitting his brows, "because that's almost exactly what really happened to us."

Sir Hubert Wotton showed a certain reticence and deliberate vagueness about the official details of the story; even in telling it after so many years to an intimate friend. In England especially, there are enormous events which never get into the newspapers, and are apparently intended never to get into the history-books. It may be enough to say here that there was at one time under the surface, but very near to the surface, a conspiracy aiming at a *coup d'état*, which was backed by a Continental Power of similar leanings. Gun-running, secret drilling and plans for stealing State documents were involved; and it was feared that a certain number of minor officials had been corrupted or converted by the conspirators. Hence, when it was a question of sending certain very private official documents (about the nature of which Wotton remained somewhat hazy to the end) from one of the great northern ports to a particular Government department in London, the first Council was a very small and select one, presided over by Sir Hubert and held in the smaller office of Mr. Pond. Indeed, Mr. Pond was the official in charge of the job. The only other person permanently present was one of the first officials from Scotland Yard; Wotton had brought his clerk with him to arrange and explain certain matters; but had later made an excuse for sending the man out on an errand. Dyer, the detective from the Yard, a heavy-shouldered, hard-headed person with a toothbrush moustache, explained methodically, if a little mechanically, the precautions and arrangements he would consider necessary for protecting the transport of the papers to their destination. He wanted an armoured car with a machine-gun, a certain number of men carrying concealed arms, a police search of everybody involved in first dispatching and in finally receiving the box or parcel—and several other conditions of the kind.

"Pond will think all this terribly expensive," said Wotton, with a sad smile. "Pond is quite the Old Liberal in the matter of economy and retrenchment. But he will agree that we are all bound to show particular care in this case."

"N-no," said Mr. Pond, pursing his lips dubiously. "I don't think I should show any particular care in this case."

"Not show any particular care!" repeated the astonished Wotton.

"I certainly shouldn't *show* it," said Mr. Pond. "In such cases, nobody of sense would take such particular precautions, any more than anybody would send an important letter by registered post."

"Well, you must pardon my dullness," said Sir Hubert, "but, as a matter of fact, I have heard of people sending an important letter by registered post."

"It is done, I believe," said Mr. Pond, with distant disparagement. "But that is when you are trying to prevent a letter being lost. Just now you are trying to prevent a letter being found."

"That sounds rather interesting," said Dyer, with some restrained amusement.

"Don't you see? It's quite simple," answered Pond. "If you want to prevent a document from being dropped down a drain, or thrown into a dustbin, or used to light the fire or to make a bird's nest, or any other accident of neglect, then it is a good thing to draw attention to it, by stamping or sealing or safeguarding it in some particular way. But if you want to prevent it from being tracked and spotted and snatched out of your hands, by violence or stratagem, then it's the worst thing in the world to mark it in a particular way. Registration, for instance, doesn't mean that your messenger can't be knocked on the head or have his pocket picked. It only means that your messenger or his department can be held responsible; may have to apologize or compensate. But you don't want apologies or compensations; you want the letter. I should say it would be far safer from a watchful enemy, if it were unmarked and sent along with a thousand others looking exactly the same."

It is a tribute to the essential shrewdness, underlying the apparent woodenness of Wotton and Dyer, that the paradox of Pond prevailed. The documents, however, were too bulky to be treated as ordinary letters; and after some discussion, they were placed in one of a large number of white wooden boxes, light and not very large, which were in general use for sending chocolate and other provisions to the army or navy or some branches of the public service. The only part of his original program on which the hard-headed Dyer continued to insist was that of putting guards and searchers at essential points of the route of travel.

"I suppose there'll be some damned fuss about it afterwards," he said, "and people will pester us about interfering with the liberty of the subject. We're handicapped in this confounded constitutional country. Now if we were in——"

He shut his mouth rather sharply, as a discreet knock sounded on the door, and Sir Hubert's clerk glided in to say he had discharged his commission. Sir Hubert did not see him at first, his frowning gaze being fixed on the railway-map of the route to be pursued; and Dyer happened at the moment to be examining very closely the white deal box, which had already been selected and sent in as a sample. But Mr. Pond noticed the clerk; and could not help thinking that he was rather worth noticing. He was a young man named Franks, with fair hair correctly flattened, and neat enough in figure and costume; but his wide face had that indescribable look which is sometimes seen, of which we can only say that it suggests the large head on the little figure of a dwarf, or perhaps that sunken between the shoulders of a hunchback; the face is not normal, even upon a normal figure. But the other causes which arrested Mr. Pond's eye for a moment were, first, the fact that the clerk was noticeably ill at ease when he silently handed papers to his superior; and, last but not least, that he had started visibly when he saw the detective from Scotland Yard.

The second Council, if it may be called so, was held in what all agreed was the strategical centre of the whole manœuvre: a certain railway-junction in the Midlands. It so happened that the consignment of boxes, along with mailbags and similar things, had to be shifted here from one train to another, which came up afterwards to the same platform. It was at this point that there was most possibility of any interference from outside; and it is to be feared that Dyer stretched several points in his reluctant compromise with the British Constitution, in the matter of police orders which stopped, detained or examined persons attempting to enter or leave the station.

"I have told our people they mustn't even let *us* out of the station," he said, "without close examination, for fear somebody should have a fancy for dressing up as Mr. Pond."

"It has quite a festive sound, so near Christmas," said Mr. Pond dolefully. "So I take it that for the present we must stay on the station; and one can hardly say it looks particularly festive."

Nothing, indeed, can well look more desolate than one of the numerous side platforms of an empty railway-station on a dreary winter day; unless it is the empty Third Class Waiting-Room which is provided to be a human refuge from the winter blast. Somehow the waiting-room looks even less human than the platform from which it is a refuge; hung with a few printed notices that nobody could possibly read, tables of trains or dusty plans of railways, equipped in one corner with broken pens with which nobody could write, and dried inkstands containing no ink to write with; with one dab of dull colours, the faded advertisement of an insurance company. It certainly seemed to the casual mind a godforsaken place to be spending any part of Christmas; but Mr. Pond had a stoical cheerfulness under such circumstances which rather surprised those who only knew his catlike love of comfortable domestic routine.

He entered this empty and unsightly apartment with a brisk step, stopping for a moment to stare reflectively at the dried ink and broken pens on the corner table.

"Well," he said, turning away, "they couldn't do very much with those, anyhow; but, of course, they might have pencils or fountain-pens. I'm rather glad I did it, on the whole."

"Pond," said Wotton gravely, "this is in your department anyhow; and I'm sure that Dyer will agree that we've done well to follow your advice so far. But I hope you don't mind my having a mild curiosity about what it is that you've done."

"Not at all," replied Pond. "Perhaps I ought to have told you about it before. Very likely I ought to have done it before. But just after you'd been good enough to let me have my own way, about sending it along with all the other stuff in plain identical boxes, I sat down and had a hard think about what would be the next best precaution following on that. I'm pretty certain that if it had been taken in a special car by armed men, that car would have been wrecked and those armed men perhaps robbed by force of arms; anyhow, there was too much of a risk of it. There's a much more elaborate gangster organization working against us already than most people have any notion of; and to multiply purchases and preparations is to multiply clues and transactions for their spies to trail. But I don't think the gangs could possibly get in here, especially now that the police are holding the gates of all these stations like fortresses. An isolated man or so could do very little against them. But what could an isolated man do?"

"Well," said Wotton rather impatiently. "What could he do?"

"As I say," continued Mr. Pond calmly, "I sat down and had a good think about what a spy or stray intruder might do, in a quiet way without any noise of battle, murder or sudden death, if he did manage somehow to spot the right box. So I got on to the private telephone to headquarters; and told them to see that the postal and transport authorities held up every one of the boxes or packages on which the address seemed to have been altered; anything crossed out or anything substituted. A man might conceivably snatch a moment to re-direct a box to some of his friends in London; though he could never take the box out of the station without being searched. That's what I did; and it was these broken-down penholders that reminded me of it. It's a pretty broken-down place to spend Christmas in, as you say; they have given us a sort of a fire, which is more than some waiting-rooms do; but it looks as if it were dying of depression; and I don't wonder."

He stirred up the neglected fire, making quite a creditable blaze, with his usual instinct for the comforts of life; then he added: "I hope you don't disagree with that second precaution of mine."

"No; I think that also is a very sensible precaution; though I hope there is no chance of anybody hitting on the right box, even by accident." Hubert Wotton frowned a moment at the renewed flame and the dancing sparks, and then said gloomily, "This is about the time when people at Christmas are going to the pantomime. Or, at any rate, to the pictures."

Mr. Pond nodded; he seemed to be suddenly smitten with a fit of abstraction. At last he said:

"I sometimes wonder whether things weren't better when pictures meant the pictures in the fire, instead of the pictures on the film."

Sir Hubert Wotton gruffly suggested, in a general way, that the dingy fire in a Third Class Waiting-Room was not one in which he would prefer to look for pictures.

"The fire pictures, like the cloud pictures," went on Mr. Pond, "are just incomplete enough to call out the imagination to complete them. Besides," he added, cheerfully poking the fire, "you can stick a poker into the coals and break them up into a different picture; whereas, if you push a great pole through the screen because you don't like the face of a film-star, there is all sorts of trouble."

Dyer, who had stamped out on to the platform during this imaginative interlude, returned at this moment with highly practical news. By exploring many tunnels, and scouring many platforms on that labyrinthine junction, he had found that there really was a remote refreshment-room, in which it was possible to have some sort of lunch; which had been a silent problem for all three of the officials involved.

"I'll stay on this platform," he said; "in fact I shall stay on this platform all night if necessary. This is my particular job. But you go and get your lunch first and come back; and I'll see if I can get some afterwards. Never mind about the trains; I've arranged for all that; and, anyhow, I shall be there when the only possible moment of danger comes."

In fact, his last words were almost drowned in the throb and racket of the approach of the first train. They all saw the mailbags and boxes and packages duly put out on the platform; and then Wotton, a man of regular habits, who was beginning to feel rather peckish, was easily persuaded by Dyer to accept his arrangement and go in search of a bite of food. Wotton and Pond dispatched their rather meagre lunch with reasonable rapidity; but even so had occasion to quicken their footsteps as they came within sight of their own original platform; since a train, which was apparently the second train, was beginning to shift and puff out of the station; and when they rejoined their companion, the platform was already bare.

"All safe," said Dyer, with satisfaction. "I saw all the boxes and things into the van myself; and nobody's been here to interfere with them. Our main trouble is really over; and I shouldn't mind having a little lunch myself."

He grinned at them, rubbing his hands in a congratulatory manner; and as he turned towards the subterranean passages, they turned once more with the intention of returning to the hollow and smoky cell of the waiting-room.

"It does seem as if there were nothing more for us to do here," said Wotton. "It rather increases the freezing futility of this shack."

"I consider it quite a Christmas triumph," said Mr. Pond, with undiminished cheerfulness, "that we have managed to keep the fire in, anyhow. . . . Why, I believe it's begun to snow."

For some time they had noted that the afternoon, already darkening towards the early winter evening, had something of that lurid greenish light which often glows under the load of snow-clouds; a sprinkling began to fall as they went along the apparently interminable platform; and by the time they reached the austere waiting-room, its roof and doorway were powdered with silver. The fire was burning briskly inside; Dyer had evidently been keeping himself warm.

"It's devilish queer," said Wotton, "but the whole thing is really beginning to look like a Christmas card. Our dismal *salle d'attente* will soon be a parody of Father Christmas's cottage in a pantomime."

"The whole thing is like the parody of a pantomime," said Pond in a lower and more disquieted tone, "and as you say, it is very queer."

After a pause, Wotton added abruptly:

"What is worrying you, Pond?"

"I'm wondering, if not worrying," answered Pond, "about exactly what a man *would* do to intercept or misdirect that box, in a place like this, with no pens or anything. . . . Of course, there's not much in that; he might have a fountain-pen or a pencil."

"Oh, you've settled all that; you seem to be mad on pencils," said Wotton impatiently. "It comes of always blue-pencilling those everlasting proofs of yours."

"It wouldn't be a blue pencil," said Pond, shaking his head. "I was thinking of something more like a red pencil; which would mark very black indeed. But what bothers me is that there are always more ways of doing anything than you'd fancy, even in a place like this."

"But you've blocked all that already," insisted the other; "by telephoning as you did."

"Well," said Pond obstinately, "and what would they do then; if they knew I'd telephoned?"

Wotton looked puzzled; and Pond sat down in silence, stirring the fire and staring at it.

After a silence he said abruptly: "I wish Dyer were back."

"What do you want him now for?" asked his friend. "I should say he'd earned a little late lunch. As far as I can see, he's finished the business; and it's all over here."

"I fear," said Pond, without taking his head out of the fireplace, "that it's only just going to begin."

There was another silence of growing mystification, like the gathering darkness outside. And then Pond observed suddenly:

"I suppose we've come back to the right platform."

Wotton's face only expressed the stolid stupefaction natural under the circumstances; but in his depths, which were deeper than some supposed, an unearthly chill touched him for the first time. Nightmare stirred in its sleep; not the mere practical perplexity of a problem, but all those doubts beyond reason which revolve round place and time. Before he could speak, Pond added:

"This is a different shaped poker."

"What the devil do you mean?" exploded Wotton at last. "They have locked up the station; and there is nobody on it but ourselves; except that girl in the bar. You don't imagine she has put a new set of furniture and fire-irons in all the waiting-rooms?"

"No," said Mr. Pond. "I didn't say a new poker. I said a new shape of poker."

Almost as he spoke, he leapt away from the fireplace, leaving the poker in the fire, and ran to the doorway, craning out his head and listening. His companion listened also; and recognized as an objective reality, which was no nightmare, a noise of scrambling footsteps somewhere on the platform. But, when they ran out, the platform appeared to be perfectly empty, now a blank and solid table of snow; and they began to realize that the noise came from underneath their feet. Looking over the railing, they saw that the whole raised woodwork of the station was intercepted at one point by a belt of grassy embankment, very grey and discoloured with the smoke; they were just in time to see a dark lean figure scramble up this bank and dive under the platform, in such a manner that he was able the next moment to crawl out on the line. Then he calmly mounted the platform, and stood there like a passenger waiting for a train.

Apart from the fact that the stranger had practically burgled the station, against such very special difficulties, Wotton's mind, already full of suspicions, decided at a glance that he was very much of a dark horse. Curiously enough, he looked a little like a horse, having a long equine visage and a strange sort of stoop; he was swarthy and haggard and his hollow eyes were such dense patches of shadow that it was a sort of shock to realize that the eyes within were glaring. He was dressed with the last extreme of shabbiness, in a long threadbare and almost ragged waterproof; and they thought they had never seen before a face and figure so symbolic of desolation and dreary tragedy. It seemed to Wotton that he himself had his first real glimpse of those depths in which despair manufactures the many revolutionary movements which it had been his duty to combat; but, of necessity, his duty prevailed.

He stepped up to the man, asking him who and what he was, and why he had thus evaded the police blockade. The man appeared to ignore the other questions for the moment; but in answer to the question about what he was, his tragic lantern-jaw moved and emitted a very unexpected reply.

"I am a Clown," he said in a depressed voice.

At this answer Mr. Pond seemed to start with altogether a new sort of surprise. He had ruminated on the puzzles hitherto, like one pursuing the study of things which some might find surprising, but at which he himself was no longer very much surprised. But he gaped helplessly at this as a man does at a miracle; or still more, in a case like this, at a coincidence. Then another and yet more undignified change came over him. It can only be said that, having begun by goggling, he ended by giggling.

"Oh, Lord, this is an extra!" he exclaimed, and seemed once more broken up by almost senile laughter. "This has nothing to do with the story; but it is a marvellous addition to the pantomime. I always noticed that the chief features in the pantomime had nothing to do with the story."

But Sir Hubert Wotton was having no more for the moment of Mr. Pond's fanciful mysteries; least of all, of the last and most mysterious, the mystery of his mirth. He had already begun to cross-examine the stranger in the style of the police; and the stranger stood up to him with gloomy but unshaken lucidity. His name, by his own account, was Hankin, and he was a public entertainer who also gave private entertainments; who was, indeed, only too glad to give any entertainments, in the depressed condition of his state of livelihood. He had an engagement to perform as clown at a children's party that evening, and had insisted on the necessity of catching a particular train; nor had he been cheered by the assurance of the police at the entrance that regular trains for passengers would be running again in an hour, at a time that would make him too late for his appointment; and lose him the first few shillings he had earned in many months. He had done what many such people would probably have been glad to do, if they had had the activity and audacity, and had climbed into the station by an unguarded loophole. This statement was made with firmness and simplicity, and Pond evidently believed it; but Wotton was still smouldering with some suspicions.

"I must ask you to come with us to the waiting-room," he said. "Have you anything about you to confirm your story?"

"I haven't got my visiting-card," said the sombre Mr. Hankin. "I lost it along with my Rolls-Royce and my little castle in Scotland. But you can see me in my resplendent and fashionable evening-dress, if you like. I think that ought to convince you."

The man was carrying a shabby and misshapen bag, which he lugged along to the waiting-room; and there, before the staring eyes of Wotton, he stripped off his waterproof and appeared in a sort of white circus dress, but for retaining his shabby boots and trousers. Then he dived into the bag and brought out a monstrous grinning and glaring white mask, picked out with red ornaments, and fitted it on his head. And there, solid and seemingly incredible before their eyes, was the genuine clown of the old-fashioned pantomime, such as they had been discussing.

"He came up through a trapdoor, I suppose we must say," murmured the awestruck Mr. Pond. "But I feel as if he had fallen out of the sky like the snow. Fate or the fairies have added this final touch; see how they built up gradually round us the whole palace of pantomime in this wilderness; first the firelight and then the snow and now the only original 'Here We Are Again!' Such a cosy happy Christmas! Screams of joy from all the tiny tots. . . . Oh, my God, how ghastly it all is!"

His friend looked at him and received a second shock in realizing that the bearded face, though it still wore the elfish look of its first amusement at the accident, was in fact terribly pale.

"And the ghastliest part of it," said Mr. Pond, "is that I am going to complete your costume, Sir."

He suddenly plucked out the poker, from where it was standing in the fire, and it emerged already red-hot. He handed it politely to the Clown.

"I may look like a pantaloon," he said, "but this will obviously be more suitable to the Clown. This is the red-hot poker, with which you make the Policeman jump."

Wotton stared at a scene to which he had now entirely lost the clue; and in the silence that followed, the long platform outside resounded with a firm and heavy stride coming nearer and nearer. The large figure of Dyer the detective appeared framed in the doorway; and he stood as if turned to stone by what he saw.

Wotton was not astonished at his astonishment. He presumed that it was an astonishment like his own, at the irrelevant intrusion of the pantomime figure. But Pond was watching more closely; and for Pond that moment was the confirmation of the creeping suspicion that had worked its way into his mind for the last hour or so. Nobody could have been surprised at Dyer staring at the Clown. But Dyer was not staring at the Clown. Nor was Dyer merely astonished; perhaps the most astonishing thing was that he was not exactly astonished. He was staring only at the poker; and he obviously saw nothing funny about it. His face was distorted by almost demoniac fear and fury; and he looked at the red pantomime poker rather as if it had been the flaming sword of an accusing angel.

"Yes, it's the red-hot poker," said Pond, in a low and almost forced voice, "and it does make the policeman jump."

The policeman jumped; he jumped back three paces, and as he leapt he loosened a big official revolver and fired at Mr. Pond again and again; the shocks of explosion shaking the thin shanty in which they stood. The first shot buried itself in the wall about an inch from Mr. Pond's dome-like forehead; the other four went rather wild; for Wotton and the stranger had woken up to the situation and were struggling with the would-be assassin, and forcing his hand away. Finally, he managed to wrench his hand loose again and twist the pistol inwards upon himself; the body of the big man stiffened in their arms; and Dyer of the detective service lay dead on the floor before the dancing fire.

The explanation of events was given by Mr. Pond some time later; for his first action after the catastrophe left no time for explanations. He had repeatedly, at intervals, looked at the clock in the waiting-room, and seemed satisfied; but he was leaving nothing to chance. He darted out of the door, raced down the platform, and found his way to the telephone-box he had used earlier in the day. He came out wiping his brow, in spite of the cold; but wearing a smile of relative relief in the midst of the tragedy. When asked what he was doing, he answered simply: "I was telephoning a description of the package. It'll be all right now; they will hold it up."

"Do you mean *the* package?" asked Wotton. "I thought that was just like all the rest."

"I'll tell you all about it presently," replied Pond. "Let us go and take a polite farewell of the public entertainer, who has given us such a delightful entertainment. I really think we ought to give him a fiver or so in compensation."

Wotton was very much the gentleman, in the more generous sense, and he heartily agreed to this; and, though it was difficult for the melancholy man with the horse-face to produce anything nearer to a laugh than a neigh, he was manifestly much cheered internally and his gaunt face was cracked with a crooked smile. Then, by way of finishing their Christmas feast on this curious scene of festivity, the two friends adjourned to the one and only refreshment-room and sat down behind two tall glasses of beer; having no taste for warming their hands at that rather too blood-red fire that still burned in the sinister waiting-room.

"It was curious you were able to corner Dyer like that," said Wotton. "I never had a thought of him."

"I never had a thought of him either," said Pond, "and he cornered himself, just as he killed himself. I fancy many conspirators are really chasing themselves into corners like that. Don't you see that he locked himself into a logical prison, when he would empty and close the whole station, to impress us with his efficiency. By the way, I ought to have guessed there was a double meaning in his dictatorial ways and demands to override the Constitution; he was talking exactly as our enemies and their foreign friends talk. But the point is this. I wasn't thinking about him particularly; I never thought of him at all until I found him wandering about inside the logical square or enclosure, like a rectangle in geometry. I was thinking all the time about one thing: what would these people probably do to divert or intercept the box, now that they could hardly do it by direct attack or anything that made a noise? I was more and more convinced they would try to redirect it somehow, so that its going normally through the post would serve them and not us. So I warned the authorities to stop all altered addresses on suspicion; and I said to myself: What will the enemy do now? What can he do, shut up in this enormous shed, bare of all conveniences and appliances? But don't you see that with that very thought came the overpowering suspicion of who the enemy was?

"Nobody was there but you and Dyer when I said I had 'phoned to stop all altered addresses. I know in a mystery story I should have to allow for the station being thronged with silent eavesdroppers, a spy up the chimney and another crawling out of the luggage; but in practical life it doesn't happen. We heard the one and only intruder, when he began to scramble up from the street. The man who did hear it was Dyer; and notice that he almost immediately wandered away up the platform, professing to find our luncheon place for us; but really striding up and down and brooding upon what the devil he should do next, for I am sure his original plan had been to alter the address as I suggested. Was there anything else in that bare beastly place he could use for the same purpose, or another similar purpose? There was. But I never guessed what it was, until I came back to the waiting-room and happened to look at the poker. I saw it was twisted at a slightly different angle; that could only mean it had been red-hot and hammered half crooked like a horseshoe on the anvil. And then, of course, I realized that a red-hot poker would serve as well as a pen or pencil, or rather better, for altering an inscription on a wooden box. A pen could only cross it out; but a poker could burn it out. Managed neatly, it might well remove all trace of there ever having been any label or previous inscription at all. But it would do a great deal more than that. The clown is not the only artist who wields a poker; there is the whole elegant craft called poker-work. It would be quite easy to change the whole appearance of a white deal box, so that it would no longer be classed with the other boxes; running a black border round it, covering it with a pattern, perhaps blackening it almost entirely. Then in one blank space left he would brand the address he wanted it to reach, very plain in black block letters, avoiding incidentally all the dangers of being traced by handwriting. The thing would have gone through the post to that address as a separate thing in an ordinary way; and our scheme for posting it in an ordinary way would have recoiled on our heads. As it was, I was just in time to describe the poker-work box and stop it. I made a silly joke about a red pencil marking black; but even then I had barely begun to suspect Dyer; I'm ashamed to say the only person I began by suspecting was your unfortunate clerk Franks, who is rather exceptionally innocent."

"Franks!" exclaimed Wotton. "Why on earth did you suspect him?"

"Because I was an ass," said Pond, "and much more like a Pantaloon than you may imagine. He's a queer-looking fellow; but I ought to have known that suffering sort of look is more often conscientiousness than unconscientiousness. But where I was a priceless ass was when I looked at the suspect instead of looking at the detective. At that moment, Dyer was holding the box up, looking at it very closely; and Franks, from the other side, could see that he made a minute mark on it, very unobtrusively; so that he would know it again. Franks knew about the box scheme; and seeing that very swift and furtive act, he started and stared; and I don't wonder. In fact, Franks was the real detective and was far ahead of me, for I hadn't suspected Dyer at all. Not till, so to speak, I actually found him like a burglar on the premises. I might say on the logical premises." He coughed slightly. "Pray excuse the pun."

"Well," said Captain Gahagan, when Wotton had told him the story long afterwards. "My favourite character in your drama is the Clown. He is so irrelevant. I am like that myself. I am so irrelevant."

"You are," said Sir Hubert Wotton, and resumed the study of his documents.

"He is like the Clown in Shakespeare," went on Gahagan with unchanged buoyancy. "The Clown in Shakespeare seems to be there by accident unconnected with the story and yet he is the chorus of the tragedy. The Fool is like a fantastic dancing flame lighting up the features and furniture of the dark house of death. Perhaps we may connect Pond and Polonius after all." And he continued to illustrate his theory of the buffoons in Shakespeare, a dramatic poet to whom he was fervently devoted, quoting large portions of the plays in question in the old oratorical Irish fashion, to the no small aid and acceleration of the business of the department, busy at the moment with oppressing and delicate problems about American claims concerning the commerce of Vancouver.

THE UNMENTIONABLE MAN

MR. POND was eating oysters; a serious and improving sight. His friend Wotton did not care for oysters; saying he could not see the sense of swallowing something you could hardly taste. He often said he could not see the sense of things; and was deaf to the wistful questions of his friend Gahagan, about whether he might perhaps see the nonsense. There was no nonsense about Sir Hubert Wotton; and there was a great deal of nonsense about Captain Gahagan. Gahagan enjoyed oysters, yet one could not say he cared for them, being a careless card; and the towers of oyster-shells before him showed that he had enjoyed them rapidly and recklessly, as a mere *hors d'œuvre*. But Mr. Pond was really caring for oysters: counting them like sheep and consuming them with the utmost care.

"It is comparatively little known," observed Gahagan, "that Pond actually is an oyster. He builds up out of oysters the permanent type or image. Hasty naturalists (I need only name the impetuous Pilk) have repeated the report that he resembles a fish. But what a fish! It was left to the researches of Nibbles, in his epoch-making work, *Pondus Ostroanthropus, or The Human Oyster Revealed*, to give our friend his high and rightful rank in the biological order. I need not trouble you with the arguments. Pond wears a beard. He and the oyster alone confront the world of modern fashions with such a decoration. When he shuts up his head he is as close as an oyster. When he persuades us to swallow something, it is only afterwards (as we often agreed) that we realize what a monster of the deep we have swallowed. But, above all, within that oyster are the paradoxes; which are pearls of great price." And he waved a glass towards Pond, as if concluding a speech and proposing a toast.

Mr. Pond bowed gravely and swallowed another oyster. "As a matter of fact, I was reminded of something relevant to the discussion by the sight of the oysters; or, more strictly, of the oyster-shells. This question of deporting dangerous characters, even when they are only suspects, has some curious and baffling problems. I remember one rather queer case, in which a government had to consider the deporting of a desirable alien——"

"I suppose you mean an undesirable alien," said Wotton.

Mr. Pond digested another oyster with an unobtrusive gulp and continued: ". . . the deporting of a desirable alien; and it found that the difficulties were really quite insurmountable. I assure you I am describing the peculiar position in perfectly appropriate terms. If any point might be questioned, it is not so much the word 'desirable' as the word 'alien.' In one sense, he might have been described as a very desirable native."

"Oysters," said Gahagan mournfully. "The Mind is still brooding upon oysters. They are certainly very desirable natives."

"If he was not desirable, he was at least desired," continued the unruffled Pond. "No, my dear Gahagan, when I say 'desired,' I do not mean 'wanted by the police.' I mean that nearly everybody wanted him to stay, and that was why it seemed obvious that he must go. He was something which, without profanity, I trust, I might call the desire of all nations; or what poets have described as the world's desire. And yet he was not deported. Although he was desired, he was not deported. That is the only real paradox."

"Oh," said the staring Wotton. "So that's the real paradox."

"You should remember something of the case, Wotton," went on Mr. Pond. "It was about that time when we went over to Paris together about a rather delicate——"

"Pond in Paris," murmured Gahagan. "Pond in his Pagan Youth, when (as Swinburne says so beautifully) 'Love was the pearl of his oyster and Venus rose red out of wine.' "

"Paris is on the way to many capitals," replied Pond with diplomatic reserve. "In any case, there is no need to define the precise scene of this little international problem. Suffice it to say that it was one of those many modern States in which a Republic, resting on representative and democratic claims, has now long replaced a Monarchy which disappeared somehow amid all the modern wars and revolutions. Like many such, it did not find all its troubles were over with the establishment of political equality; in face of a world deeply disturbed about economic equality. When I went there, a strike in the transport services had brought the life of the capital to a deadlock; the Government was accused of being under the influence of a millionaire named Kramp, who controlled the lines involved; and the crisis was the more alarming because it was insisted (on the Government side) that the strike was secretly engineered by the famous terrorist, Tarnowski, sometimes called the Tiger of Tartary, who having been exiled from his own part of Eastern Europe, was believed to be spreading conspiracies from some unknown hiding-place in the West." Mr. Pond then proceeded to narrate his little experience, which, when purged of Gahagan's interruptions and Pond's somewhat needless exactitudes, was substantially this.

Pond was rather lonely in this strange capital; for Wotton had gone elsewhere on the other delicate mission; and, having no friends, Pond picked up only a few acquaintances. But he picked up at least three acquaintances who turned out to be rather interesting in various ways. The first case was commonplace enough, it might seem; consisting merely of talking to a bookseller who was otherwise a fairly ordinary shopkeeper, but well acquainted with early eighteenth-century scientific books; and the period was a hobby with Pond. Otherwise Mr. Huss was highly *bourgeois*, with a heavy frockcoat and long, antiquated whiskers which met under his chin in a patriarchal beard. When he went outside his shop, which was not often, he wore a funereal chimney-pot hat. Scientific studies seemed to have left in him the sort of stagnant atheism that is at once respectable and depressing; but beyond that there was nothing to distinguish him from countless Continental shopkeepers. The next man with whom Pond fell into any sort of conversation, in a café, was much more vigorous and vigilant, and belonged to a younger world. But he also was very serious; a dark, strenuous young man who was a Government official actually believing in the Government; or at least in the principles of the Government; and he was the sort of man who thinks first about principles. He denounced the strike and even the trade union; not because he was a snob, for he lived as simply as a workman; but because he really did believe in the old individualistic theory of what he called free contract. The type is almost unknown in England; the theory is more common in America. But nobody who looked at the baldish, rather corrugated brow that bulged between the streaks of black hair, and the anxious, though angry, eyes, could doubt that he was in fanatical good faith. His name was Marcus, and he held a minor Government office, in which he could survey with satisfaction the principles of the Republic, without being admitted to its counsels. It was while talking outside a café with this second acquaintance, that Mr. Pond became conscious of the third, who was by far the most extraordinary of the three.

This man was a sort of magnet for the human eye; Pond soon realized that this was true of everybody's eyes and not merely his own. One way or another, a current of communications seemed to be always circling round the little table where the man sat smoking a cigarette and sipping black coffee and benedictine. At the moment when Pond first saw him, a group of young men was breaking up after some tangle of talk and laughter; they seemed to have stopped by the table merely for the sake of the talk. The next moment a string of gutter-children invaded his solitude and received the pieces of sugar not used for his coffee; then a hulking and rather sulky-looking labourer came up and talked to him, for a much longer time than any of the others. Strangest of all, a lady, of the stiff aristocratic sort seldom seen outside the house in such countries, actually got out of a carriage and stood staring at the strange gentleman; and then got into the carriage again. These things alone might have led Pond to look at the person in question; but in fact, for some reason or other, he had looked at him with great curiosity from the first.

The man wore a wide white hat and a rather shabby dark blue suit; he had a high-bridged nose and a pale yellow beard brushed to a point. He had long, bony, but elegant, hands, on one of which was a ring with a stone coloured like a kingfisher, the only spot of luxury on what was otherwise a rather threadbare appearance; and in the grey shadow of the white hat his eyes shone as blue as the stone. There was nothing in his position that claimed prominence; he did not sit in the front but up against the wall of the café, just under a creeper and a fire-escape. Despite the little crowds that clustered round him, he had in the intervals an odd air of preferring to be alone. Pond made many inquiries, then and afterwards, about his name; but learnt nothing except that he was commonly called M. Louis; but whether that was his real surname, or perhaps the adaptation of some foreign surname, or whether his queer and eccentric popularity led everybody to use his Christian name, did not very clearly emerge.

"Marcus," said Mr. Pond to his young companion, "who *is* this man?"

"Everybody knows him and nobody knows who he is," replied Marcus in a rather grating voice. "But I'm jolly well going to find out."

As he spoke, the hawkers of the revolutionary paper, published by the strikers and conspicuous by being printed on vivid scarlet paper, were distributing it among a considerable number of purchasers in the crowd outside the café; a black block thus rapidly diversified with blots of blood-red colour. Some, indeed, looked at the paper only to jeer at it; some with a colder curiosity; perhaps only a few with the respect of real sympathizers. Among those reading it with detachment, but not apparently with definite disapproval, was the gentleman with the beard and the blue ring: M. Louis.

"Well," said Marcus, with a darkening brow. "Let them. It's their last chance, I suppose."

"Why, what do you mean?" inquired Pond.

The brow of Marcus became still more corrugated and troubled; at length he said in a gruff and rather reluctant manner: "I'm bound to say I don't approve of it myself. I can't see how the Republic can reconcile it with its liberal principles to suppress newspapers. But they're going to suppress that newspaper. They've been a good deal goaded. I don't believe the Prime Minister himself really likes the suppression; but the Minister of the Interior is a fiery little devil and generally gets his own way. Anyhow, they're going to raid the offices with police to-morrow; and that's probably the last issue."

M. Marcus proved himself a true prophet, so far as concerned the general situation next morning.

There had apparently been another issue; but if it had ever been displayed it had not been successfully distributed; the police had seized all copies of it everywhere; and the black-clad *bourgeoisie* sitting outside the café were now blameless and unspotted with any hues of blood; save in one corner under the fire-escape and the creeper, where M. Louis was reading his copy of the sanguinary sheet in complete indifference to the change. Some of those around him eyed him slightly askance; and Pond specially noticed Mr. Huss, the bookseller, complete with black top-hat and white whiskers, seated at a table close by and eyeing the reader of the red paper with bristling suspicion.

Marcus and Pond took their seats at their own original table; and even as they did so, a contingent of police came by, marching very rapidly, cleaning up the streets. There marched with them, with yet more furious rapidity, a squat, square man with arrogant moustaches, wearing an official decoration and flourishing an umbrella like a sabre. This was the eminent and highly militant Dr. Koch, the Minister of the Interior; he had been presiding over the police raid, and his rolling eye instantly spotted the one red spot in the corner of the crowded café. He planted himself before M. Louis; and shouted as if on parade:

"You are forbidden to read that paper. It contains direct incitement to crime."

"And how," asked M. Louis courteously, "and how can I discover this deplorable fact except by reading it?"

Something in that polite tone seemed, for some odd reason, to cause the Minister of the Interior to fly, as the phrase goes, right off the handle. Pointing his umbrella at the man in the café, he vociferated with a violent distinctness:

"You could be arrested, you could be deported; and you know why. Not for all that bloody nonsense. You don't need that scrap of a scarlet rag to mark you out among decent citizens."

"Because my own sins are as scarlet," said the other, gently inclining his head, "the scandal of my presence here is indeed highly scandalous. And why don't you arrest me?"

"You wait and see whether we arrest you," said the Minister grinding his teeth. "Anyhow, you shan't arrest us or hold up the whole machinery of society by a trick like this. Do you think we will let that sort of dirty little red rusty nail in the road stop all the wheels of progress?"

"And do you think," answered the other sternly, "that all the wheels of your sort of progress have ever done anything yet but grind the faces of the poor? No; I have not the honour of being one of the citizens of your State; one of those happy, joyful, well-fed, wealthy citizens one sees standing about in the street, on whom you wage war by hunger. But I am not a subject of any foreign State; and you will have quite a peculiar difficulty in deporting me back to my own country."

The Minister took one furious step forward; and then stopped. Then he walked off twirling his moustaches, as if suddenly forgetting the very existence of the other; and followed in the track of the police.

"There seem to be a number of mysteries here," said Mr. Pond to his friend. "First, why should he be deported? Second, why shouldn't he be deported?"

"I don't know," said Marcus, and stood up stiff and frowning.

"All the same," said Mr. Pond, "I am beginning to have a sort of fancy about who he is."

"Yes," said Marcus grimly, "and I'm beginning to have a fancy about what he is. Not a nice fancy." And he strode abruptly away from the table and up the street alone.

Mr. Pond remained seated in a condition of profound thought. After some minutes he rose and made his way towards the table where his friend the bookseller, the excellent Huss, was still seated in somewhat darkling majesty.

Even as he crossed the crowded *trottoir,* a roar broke from the street behind him, which was filling with twilight; and he realized that the great grey crowd of the strikers was on the march past, following the same route as the police who had just cleared out their offices. But the cause of the cry was more particular and even personal. The sardonic eyes of the semi-starving mob had swept the whole dark and decorous crowd of respectable people outside the café, and marked the absence of their proscribed paper; then they had suddenly perceived the familiar red flare of its fluttering pages in the hands of M. Louis, who was continuing to read it with unaltered calm. All the strikers stood still, halting and saluting like an army; and a great shout, seeming to shake the lamp-posts and little trees, went up for the one man who remained faithful to the red rag. M. Louis rose and gravely bowed to the applauding mob. Mr. Pond sat down opposite his friend the bookseller and scrutinized his whiskered face with interest.

"Well," said Mr. Pond, "our friend over there looks as if he might soon be the leader of the revolutionary party."

This remark had a rather strange effect on Mr. Huss; he started as in disorder by saying: "No, no"; controlled his countenance, and then enunciated a number of short sentences with an extraordinary exactitude.

"Myself of the *bourgeoisie,* I have yet remained apart from politics. I have taken no part in any class-war proceeding under present conditions. I have no reason to identify myself either with the protest of the proletariat or with the present phase of capitalism."

"Oh," said Mr. Pond; and an understanding began to dawn in his eyes. After a moment he said: "I apologize most sincerely, old man. I didn't know you were a Communist."

"I have confessed to nothing of the sort," said Huss heatedly; then he added abruptly: "You will say somebody has betrayed me."

"Your speech betrays you, like the Galilean," said Pond. "Every sect talks its own language. You could tell a man was a Buddhist from his way of saying he was not a Buddhist. It's no business of mine; and I won't mention it to a soul, if you prefer not. I only ventured to say that the man over there seems to be very popular with the strikers, and might lead the movement.''

''No, no, no,'' cried Huss, beating on the table with his two fists. ''Never, never, shall he lead the movement! Understand me! We are a scientific movement. We are not moral. We have done with *bourgeois* ideologies of right and wrong. We are *Realpolitik*. What helps the program of Marx is alone good. What hinders the program of Marx is alone evil. But there are limits. There are names so infamous, there are persons so infamous, that they must always be excluded from the Party.''

''You mean somebody is so wicked that he has awakened a dormant moral sense even in a Bolshevist bookseller,'' said Pond. ''Why, what has he done?''

''It is not only what he does but what he is,'' said Mr. Huss.

''Curious that you should say that,'' said Pond. ''For I have just made a sort of a guess about what he is.''

He took a newspaper-cutting from his waistcoat pocket and pushed it across to the other, remarking casually: ''You will note that Tarnowski the Terrorist is now said to be fomenting strikes and revolutions not only in this country but definitely in this capital. Well, our friend in the white hat seems to me to be rather an old hand.''

Huss was still drumming faintly on the table and obscurely muttering: ''Never, never, shall he be the leader.''

''But suppose he is the leader?'' said Pond. ''He obviously has a sort of habit of old leadership about him; a sort of gesture of authority. Isn't he going on exactly as Tarnowski the Tiger probably would go on?''

Mr. Pond may have expected to surprise the bookseller; but it was Mr. Pond who got the surprise. The effect on the bookseller was such that surprise would be a comically inadequate description. Mr. Huss stiffened and sat as still as a stone idol; but the change in the face of the graven image was appalling. It suggested some nightmare story of a man at a solitary table finding he was dining with a devil.

''My God,'' said the atheist at last, in a small, weak rather squeaky voice, ''and so you think *he* is Tarnowski!'' And with that, the bookseller in the top-hat suddenly went off into hoots of hollow laughter, like the dismal noises of an owl, shrill and monotonous and apparently to be repeated indefinitely without control.

"Well," interrupted Pond, mildly exasperated, "how can you possibly know that he is not Tarnowski?"

"Only because I am Tarnowski," said the bookseller, with sudden sobriety. "You say you are not a spy. But you can betray me if you choose."

"I assure Your Excellency," said Mr. Pond, "that I am not a spy or even, what is worse, a gossip. I am only a tourist who is not talkative and a traveller who tells no traveller's tales. Besides, I owe a debt to Your Excellency, for having illuminated my mind with an important principle. I never saw it so clearly before. A man always says exactly what he means; but especially when he hides it."

"That," observed the other with guttural slowness, "is what I think you call a paradox."

"Oh, don't say that," groaned Mr. Pond. "Everybody in England says that. And I have honestly no notion of what it means."

"But in that case," said Mr. Pond to himself, "who on earth *is* the man in the white hat? What crime has he committed? What crime is it for which he can be arrested or deported? Or again, what crime is it for which he *can't* be arrested or deported?"

It was in a burst of splendid sunshine, on the following morning, that Pond sat at his little table in the café ruminating on the renewed difficulties of the problem. The sun gave a sort of golden gaiety to a scene that had lately looked rather sombre, and even black, bloodshot with the glimpses of the Bolshevist journal. In the social sense at least, there seemed to be a clearance in the storm, of the strikers if not the strike; the threat of riots had been outmanœuvred; and the police were picketed at intervals down the street; but seemed in the tranquil sunshine as harmless as the toy trees and the painted lamp-posts. Mr. Pond felt an irrational return of that vague exhilaration which an Englishman sometimes feels in the mere fact of being abroad; the smell of the French coffee affected him as some are affected by the smell of hayfields or the sea. M. Louis had resumed his amiable hobby of distributing sugar to the *gamins;* and the very shape of those oblong blocks of beetroot-sugar pleased Mr. Pond in the same manner. He had a hazy feeling that he was looking at the scene through the eyes of one of the children. Even the *gendarmes* posted along the pavement amused him in a merely nonsensical manner, as if they had been dolls or dummies in some delightful puppet-play; their cocked hats carrying a vague memory of the beadle in a Punch-and-Judy show. Through all this coloured comedy there advanced the rigid figure of M. Marcus, with a visage which announced vividly that that political Puritan did not believe in puppet-shows.

"Well," he said, glaring at Pond with a sort of controlled rage, "I fancy I can guess the truth about *him*."

Pond made polite inquiries; and was answered by an unexpectedly ugly and jeering laugh.

"What sort of man is it," asked Marcus, "who is received everywhere with bows and smiles? Who is it to whom everybody is always so courteous and complimentary? What generous Friend of the People? What holy Father of the Poor? Deported! That sort of fellow ought to be hanged."

"I fear I do not understand anything yet," answered Pond mildly, "except that for some reason he cannot even be deported."

"Looks very patriarchal, doesn't he, sitting in the sunshine and playing with the children? It was darker last night and I caught him in a darker piece of business. . . . Listen to this, first of all. It was at the end of dusk, yesterday evening; and but for myself, he was alone in the café; I don't think he saw me; but I don't know if he would care. There drove up a dark, closely curtained carriage; and that lady we saw once before got out; a very grand lady, I am sure, though I fancy not so rich as she had been. She had an interview with this man, in which she actually went on her knees to him on the muddy pavement, begging him for something; and he only sat there and smiled. What sort of a man is it who sees ladies grovelling before him and only grins like a demon and doesn't even take off his hat? What sort of man is it who can play the Sultan in society and be sure that everybody will smile and be polite? Only the very basest sort of criminal."

"In plain words," said Mr. Pond, "you mean he ought to be arrested because he's a blackmailer. You also mean he can't be arrested because he's a blackmailer."

For the first time the rage of Marcus seemed mixed with a sort of embarrassment, almost amounting to shame, as he looked down scowling at the table.

"It has no doubt occurred to you," proceeded Pond placidly, "that the second inference involves some suggestions that are rather delicate; especially if I may say so, for a man in your position."

Marcus remained in a silence swollen with anger; then at last he broke out abruptly, as if beyond control: "I'll swear the Prime Minister is perfectly honest."

"I do not think," said Mr. Pond, "that I have ever regaled you with any scandals about the Prime Minister."

"And I can't believe the little doctor is really in it," went on Marcus savagely. "I've always thought it was just sincerity that made him spluttering and spiteful. It was just trying to be straight amid all this——"

"All this what?" asked Mr. Pond.

Marcus turned in his chair with an abrupt gesture of the elbow, saying: "Oh, you don't understand."

"On the contrary," replied Pond. "I think I do understand."

There was a lengthy silence and then Pond resumed:

"I understand the horrid truth that you yourself are a perfectly honourable and high-minded person and that your own problem is extremely difficult to solve. I assure you that I am quite incapable of taunting you with it. It was to the Republic, to the idea of equality and justice, that you swore loyalty; and to that you have been loyal."

"You had better say what you think," said Marcus gloomily. "You mean that I am really only serving a gang of crooks, whom any blackguard can blackmail."

"No, I will not ask you to admit that now," answered Pond. "Just now I wanted to ask you quite another question. Can't you imagine a man sympathizing with the strikers, or even being a sincere Socialist?"

"Well," replied Marcus, after a spasm of concentration, "I suppose one ought to imagine. I suppose he might hold that, the Republic resting on the Social Contract, it might supersede even free contracts."

"Thank you," said Mr. Pond with satisfaction, "that is exactly what I wanted. It is an important contribution to Pond's Law of Paradox, if I may be pardoned for expressing myself so playfully. And now let us go and talk to M. Louis."

He stood up before the astonished official, who had no apparent alternative but to follow him as he passed swiftly across the café. Some vivacious and talkative young men were taking leave of M. Louis, who courteously invited the newcomers to the empty chairs, saying something about "my young friends often enliven my solitude with their rather Socialistic views."

"I should not agree with your young friends," said Marcus curtly, "I am so old-fashioned as to believe in free contract."

"I, being older, perhaps believe in it even more," answered M. Louis smiling. "But surely it is a very old principle of law that a leonine contract is not a free contract. And it is hypocrisy to pretend that a bargain between a starving man and a man with all the food is anything but a leonine contract." He glanced up at the fire-escape, a ladder leading up to the balcony of a very high attic above. "I live in that garret; or rather on that balcony. If I fell off the balcony and hung on a spike, so far from the steps that somebody with a ladder could offer to rescue me if I gave him a hundred million francs, I should be quite morally justified in using his ladder and then telling him to go to hell for his hundred million. Hell, indeed, is not out of the picture; for it is a sin of injustice to force an advantage against the desperate. Well, all those poor men are desperate; they all hang starving on spikes. If they must not bargain collectively, they cannot bargain at all. You are not supporting contract; you are opposing all contract; for yours cannot be a real contract at all."

While the smoke of his cigarette mounted towards the balcony, Mr. Pond's eye followed it and found the balcony fitted out with what looked like a bedstead, a screen, and an old looking-glass, all very shabby. The only other object was a dusty old cross-hilted sword, such as might have come from a curiosity shop. Mr. Pond eyed this last object with considerable curiosity.

"Please permit me to play the host," said M. Louis affably. "Perhaps you would like a cocktail or something; I stick to a little benedictine."

As he turned in his chair towards the waiter, a shot rang through the café and the little glass before him lay in a star of splinters. The bullet that spilt the drink had missed the drinker by half a yard. Marcus looked wildly round; the café was deserted, for it was already late; no figure was in sight but the solid back of the *gendarme* standing outside. But Marcus went white with horror; for M. Louis made one quaint little gesture which, if it meant anything, could only mean that the policeman himself had turned for an instant and fired.

"A little reminder, perhaps, that it is time to go to bed," said M. Louis gaily. "I go up by the fire-escape and I sleep on the balcony. Doctors think so much of this open-air treatment. Well, my people have always gone to bed in public; so many tramps do, don't they? Good night, gentlemen."

He lightly scaled the iron ladder and began on the balcony, before their astonished eyes, to assume a capacious dressing-gown and prepare for slumber.

"Pond," said Marcus, "we are in a nightmare of nonsense."

"No," replied Pond, "for the first time it begins to make sense. I have been stupid; but I am beginning at last to see what it all means." After ruminating a moment, he resumed rather apologetically:

"Forgive me if I refer again to my foolish jest about Pond's Law. I think I have discovered a rather useful principle. It is this. Men may argue *for* principles not entirely their own, for various reasons; as a joke in a rag debate, or covered by professional etiquette, like a barrister, or merely exaggerating something neglected and needing emphasis; long before we come to those who do it hypocritically or for hire. A man can argue *for* principles not his own. But a man cannot argue *from* principles not his own; the first principles he assumes, even for sophistry or advocacy, will probably be his own fundamental first principles. The very language he uses will betray him. That Bolshevist bookseller professed to be a *bourgeois;* but he talked like a Bolshevist about a *bourgeois.* He talked about exploitation and the class-war. So you tried to imagine yourself a Socialist; but you did not talk like a Socialist. You talked about the Social Contract, like old Rousseau. Now our friend M. Louis was defending his sympathy with strikers and even Socialists. But he used the oldest and most traditional argument of all, older than the Roman Law. The idea about leonine contract is as old as Leo and a long sight older than Leo XIII. Therefore, he represents something even older than your Rousseau and your Revolution. I knew after five words that he was not the blackmailing blackguard of romance; and yet he is romantic. And he could be legally arrested; but only for a rather curious crime. And yet again, he cannot be arrested. He can only be assassinated.

"The blackmail charge rests on one scene, in which a lady knelt to him in the street. You argued truly that ladies in your country think so much of formality and propriety, that they could never do this except in some extreme of agony and despair. It did not occur to you that, perhaps, it might be only an extreme of formality and propriety."

Marcus began slowly: "What the devil——" And then Mr. Pond rapped out quite smartly: "And then the sword. What is a sword *for?* It's absurd to say for fighting; he wouldn't wave a mediæval sword against people shooting him with guns. If it were for duels he would have a duelling-sword; and probably two in a case. What else can you do with a sword? Well, you can swallow it; and at one time I really had a fancy he might be a conjurer. But it's too big a swallow; so is the notion. What *can* be done with a sword, but not with a spear or gun or battle-axe? Have you heard of the Accolade? Long ago a man could be knighted by any knight; but by all modern custom it can only be done——"

"Only——" began Marcus, beginning to stare.

"Only by a King," said Pond. And the young Republican sprang up rigid at the challenge.

"Yes," continued Pond, "the King has crept back among you. It is not your fault. Republics might be all right if Republicans were as honourable as you are; but you have confessed that they are not . . . and that's what he meant about going to bed in public. You know the old kings really did. But he had another reason. He had one real fear; that they might deport him secretly. They could deport him technically, of course; all these Republics have laws against Royalist claimants remaining in the realm. But if they did it publicly, he would proclaim himself and——"

"Why don't they do it publicly?" asked the Republican explosively.

"Politicians do not understand much; but politicians do understand politics," said Pond pensively. "I mean they do understand the *immediate* effect on mobs and movements. Somehow he had slipped in and started a campaign of private popularity before they even knew who he was. When once he was popular, they were helpless. How could they say: 'Yes, he is popular, he is on the side of the people and the poor; the young men accept his leadership; but he is the King and therefore he must go'? They know how horribly near the world is to answering: 'Yes; he is the King and, by God, he shall stay.' "

Mr. Pond had told this story, at somewhat greater length but in far more classic diction; and by that time had actually finished the oysters. He gazed pensively at the shells and added: "You will of course recall the meaning of the word ostracism. It meant that in ancient Athens a man was sometimes exiled merely for being important; and the votes were recorded by oyster-shells. In this case he should have been exiled for being important; but he was so very important that nobody could be told of his importance."

RING OF LOVERS

"AS I SAID BEFORE," observed Mr. Pond, towards the end of one of his lucid but rather lengthy speeches, "our friend Gahagan here is a very truthful man and tells wanton and unnecessary lies. But this very truthfulness——"

Captain Gahagan waved a gloved hand as in courteous acknowledgement of anything anybody liked to say; he had an especially flamboyant flower in his coat and looked unusually gay. But Sir Hubert Wotton, the third party at the little conference, sat up. For he followed the flow of words with tireless, intelligent attention, while Gahagan, though radiant, seemed rather abstracted; and these abrupt absurdities always brought Sir Hubert up standing.

"Say that again," he said, not without sarcasm.

"Surely that is obvious enough," pleaded Mr. Pond. "A real liar does not tell wanton and unnecessary lies. He tells wise and necessary lies. It was not necessary for Gahagan to tell us once that he had seen not one sea-serpent but six sea-serpents, each larger than the last; still less to inform us that each reptile in turn swallowed the last one whole; and that the last of all was opening its mouth to swallow the ship, when he saw it was only a yawn after too heavy a meal, and the monster suddenly went to sleep. I will not dwell on the mathematical symmetry with which snake within snake yawned, and snake within snake went to sleep, all except the smallest, which had had no dinner and walked out to look for some. It was not, I say, necessary for Gahagan to tell this story. It was hardly even wise. It is very unlikely that it would promote his worldly prospects, or gain him any rewards or decorations for scientific research. The official scientific world, I know not why, is prejudiced against any story even of one sea-serpent, and would be the less likely to accept the narrative in its present form.

"Or again, when Captain Gahagan told us he had been a Broad Church missionary, and had readily preached in the pulpits of Nonconformists, then in the mosques of Moslems, then in the monasteries of Tibet, but was most warmly welcomed by a mystical sect of Theists in those parts, people in a state of supreme spiritual exaltation who worshipped him like a god, until he found they were enthusiasts for Human Sacrifice and he was the victim. This statement was also quite unnecessary. To have been a latitudinarian clergyman is but little likely to advance him in his present profession, or to fit him for his present pursuits. I suspect the story was partially a parable or allegory. But anyhow, it was quite unnecessary and it was obviously untrue. And when a thing is obviously untrue, it is obviously not a lie."

"Suppose," said Gahagan abruptly, "suppose I were to tell you a story that really is true?"

"I should regard it with great suspicion," said Wotton grimly.

"You mean you would think I was still romancing. But why?"

"Because it would be so very like a romance," retorted Wotton.

"But don't you think," asked the Captain thoughtfully, "that real life sometimes is like a romance?"

"I think," replied Wotton, with a certain genuine shrewdness that lay very deep in him, "that I could always really tell the difference."

"You are right," said Pond; "and it seems to me the difference is this. Life is artistic in parts, but not as a whole; it's like broken bits of different works of art. When everything hangs together, and it all fits in, we doubt. I might even believe that Gahagan saw six sea-serpents; but not that each was larger than the last. If he'd said there was first a large one and then a little one and then a larger one, he might have taken us in. We often say that one social situation is like being in a novel; but it doesn't finish like the novel—at least, not the same novel."

"Pond," said Gahagan, "I sometimes think you are inspired, or possessed of a devil in a quiet way. It's queer you should say that; because my experience was just like that. With this difference; each familiar melodrama broke off; but only turned to blacker melodrama—or tragedy. Again and again, in this affair, I thought I was in a magazine story; and then it turned to quite another story. Sort of dissolving view, or a nightmare. Especially a nightmare."

"And why especially?" asked Wotton.

"It's a horrible story," said Gahagan, lowering his voice. "But it's not so horrible now."

"Of course," said Mr. Pond, nodding. "You are happy and wish to tell us a horrible story."

"And what does *that* mean?" demanded Wotton.

"It means," said Gahagan, "that I got engaged to be married this morning."

"The devil you—— I beg your pardon," said Wotton, very red in the face. "Congratulations, of course, and all that. But what has it to do with the nightmare?"

"There is a connexion," said Gahagan dreamily. "But you want the horrible story and not the happy one. Well, it was a bit of a mystery, at least to me; but I understood it at last."

"And when you've done mystifying us, you will tell us the solution?"

"No; Pond will tell you the solution," said Gahagan maliciously. "He's already puffed up because he guessed the kind of story, before he even heard it. If he can't finish the story, when he has heard it——"
He broke off and then resumed more solidly:

"It began with a dinner-party, what they call a stag-party, given by Lord Crome, following on a cocktail-party mostly given by Lady Crome. Lady Crome was a tall and swift and graceful person with a small dark head. Lord Crome was quite the reverse; he was in every way, physical and mental, a 'long-headed' person. You've heard of a hatchet-face; his was a hatchet that cut off his own head—or rather his own body; abolishing the slighter and more insignificant figure. He is an economist and he gave one the impression of being *distrait* and rather bored with all the ladies who swam about in the wake of his wonderful wife, that darting swan; and perhaps that was why he wanted the cooler society of his own sex. Anyhow, he kept some of his male guests for a little dinner after the at-home was over. I happened to be one of them; but, in spite of that, it was a select company.

"It was a select company; and yet it hardly seemed to have been selected. They were mostly well-known men, and yet it looked as if Crome had taken their names out of a hat. The first person I ran into was Captain Blande, supposed to be one of the biggest officers in the British Army, and I should think the stupidest, for any strategic purposes. Of course he looks magnificent—like a chryselephantine statue of Hercules, and about as useful in time of war. I once used the

word 'chryselephantine,' meaning gold and ivory; and he thought I
was calling him elephantine. Classical education of the *pukka sahib.*
Well, the man he was put next to was Count Kranz, the Hungarian
scientist and social reformer. He speaks twenty-seven languages,
including philosophical language. I wonder what language he talked
to Captain Blande in. Just beyond the Count was another fellow more
of Blande's sort; but darker and leaner and livelier; a fellow called
Wooster of some Bengal regiment. His language also would be
limited: the Latin verb *polo, polas, polat;* I play polo, thou playest
polo, he plays polo, or (more devastatingly) he does not play polo. But
just as polo itself was an Asiatic game, and can be traced through the
gilded jungle of Persian and Indian illuminations, so there was
something faintly Eurasian about this man Wooster; he was like a
dark-striped tiger and one could fancy him gliding through a jungle.
That pair at least looked a little more well-matched; for Kranz also
was dark and good-looking, with arched, black, Assyrian eyebrows
and a long, dark beard, spreading like a fan or the forked tail of a bird.
I sat next, and got on with Wooster pretty well; on the other side of me
was Sir Oscar Marvell, the great actor-manager, all very fine and
large, with the Olympian curls and the Roman nose. Here also there
was some lack of *rapport.* Sir Oscar Marvell didn't want to talk about
anything but Sir Oscar Marvell; and the other men didn't want to talk
about Sir Oscar Marvell at all. The three remaining men were the new
Under-Secretary for Foreign Affairs, Pitt-Palmer, a very frigid-
looking young man like the bust of Augustus Cæsar—and indeed *he*
was classical enough, and could have quoted the classics all right; one
Italian singer, whose name I could not remember, and one Polish
diplomat, whose name nobody could remember. And I was saying to
myself all the time: 'What a funny collection!' "

"I know this story," said Wotton positively. "A humorous host
collects a lot of incompatible people for the pleasure of hearing them
quarrel. Done very well in one of Anthony Berkeley's detective
stories."

"No," replied Gahagan. "I think their incompatibility was quite
accidental, and I know that Crome didn't use it to make them quarrel.
As a matter of fact, he was a most tactful host, and it would be truer to
say he prevented them from quarrelling. He did it rather cleverly, too,
by beginning to talk about heirlooms and family jewels and so on.
Different as they were, most of them were well-off, and what is called
of a good family; and it was about as close to common ground as they
could get. The Pole, who was a baldish but graceful person, with very

charming manners, and much the wittiest man at table, was giving an amusing account of the adventures of a medal of Sobieski when it fell into the hands first of a Jew, and then of a Prussian, and then of a Cossack. In contrast to the Pole, who was hairless and talkative, the Italian beyond him was silent, and rather sulky, under his bush of black hair.

" 'That's an interesting-looking ring you are wearing yourself, Lord Crome,' said the Pole politely. 'Those heavy rings are generally historic. I think I should really like to wear an episcopal ring or, better still, a Papal ring. But then there are all those tiresome preliminaries about being made Pope; it involves celibacy; and I——' And he shrugged his shoulders.

" 'Very annoying, no doubt,' said Lord Crome, smiling at him grimly. 'As for this ring here—well, it is rather interesting in a way, in that sort of family way, of course. I don't know the details, but it is obviously sixteenth century. Care to look at it?' And he slipped off his finger a heavy ring with a red stone and passed it to the Pole, who was sitting next to him. It proved on examination to be set with a cluster of extremely fine rubies and carved with a central device of a heart inside a rose. I saw it myself, since it was handed round the table; and there was some lettering in old French which meant something like 'From the lover only and only to the beloved.'

" 'A romance in your family history, I suppose?' suggested the Hungarian Count. 'And about the sixteenth century. But you do not know the story?'

" 'No,' said Crome, 'but I suppose it was, as you say, a romance in the family.'

"They began talking about sixteenth-century romances, at some length; and at last Crome asked very courteously if everybody had seen the ring."

"Oh," cried Wotton, with a deep breath, rather like a schoolboy at a conjurer's performance. "I know *this* story, anyhow. This is a magazine story, if you like! The ring wasn't returned and everybody was searched or somebody refused to be searched; and there was some awfully romantic reason for his refusing to be searched."

"You are right," said Gahagan. "Right, up to a point. The ring was not returned. We were all searched. We all insisted on being searched. Nobody refused to be searched. But the ring was gone."

Gahagan turned rather restlessly and threw an elbow over the back of his chair; after a moment he went on:

"Please don't imagine I didn't feel all you say; that we seemed to have got inside a novel; and not a very novel sort of novel. But the difference was exactly what Pond says: that the novel didn't finish properly, but seemed to go on to something else. We had just reached about the coffee stage of the dinner, while this fuss about the first discovery of the loss was being discussed. But all the nonsense about searching was really very swift and simple; and the coffee hadn't even got cold in the interlude, though Crome offered to send for some more. We all said that of course it didn't matter; but Crome summoned the butler who'd been handing it round; and they whispered together in what was obviously a rather agitated conversation. Then, just as Pitt-Palmer was lifting his coffee cup to his lips, Lord Crome sprang up stiff and bristling and called out like the crack of a whip:

" 'Gentlemen, do not touch this coffee. It is poisoned.' "

"But dash it all," interrupted Wotton, "that's a different story! I say, Gahagan, are you sure you didn't dream all this? After reading through a stack of out-of-date magazines and mixing up all the results? Of course we know the story about a whole company laid out with poison——"

"The results in this case were rather more extraordinary," said Gahagan calmly. "Most of us naturally sat like stone statues under such a thunder-bolt of a threat. But young Pitt-Palmer, with his cold, clean-cut, classical face, rose to his feet with the coffee cup in his hand and said in the coolest way:

" 'Awfully sorry; but I do hate letting my coffee get cold.'

"And he drained his cup; and, as God sees me, his face turned black or a blend of dreadful colours; and after horrible and inhuman noises, he fell down as in a fit before our eyes.

"Of course, we were not certain at first. But the Hungarian scientist had a doctor's degree; and what he reported was confirmed by the local doctor, who was sent for at once. There was no doubt that he was dead."

"You mean," said Wotton, "that the doctors agreed that he was poisoned?"

Gahagan shook his head and repeated: "I said they agreed that he was dead."

"But why should he be dead unless he was poisoned?"

"He was choked," said Gahagan; and for one instant a shudder caught his whole powerful frame.

After a silence that seemed suddenly imposed by his agitation, Wotton said at last:

"I don't understand a word you say. Who poisoned the coffee?"

"Nobody poisoned the coffee; because it wasn't poisoned," answered Gahagan. "The only reason for saying that was to make sure the coffee should remain in the cup, to be analysed just as it was. Poor Pitt-Palmer had put in a very large lump of sugar just before; but the sugar would melt. Some things do not melt."

Sir Hubert Wotton stared for some seconds into vacancy; and then his eyes began to glow with his own very real though not very rapid intelligence.

"You mean," he said, "that Pitt-Palmer somehow dropped the ring into the black coffee, where it wouldn't be seen, before he was searched. In other words, Pitt-Palmer was the thief?"

"Pitt-Palmer is dead," said Gahagan very gravely, "and it is the more my duty to defend his memory. What he did was doubtless wrong, as I have come to see more clearly than I did; but not worse than many a man has done. You may say what you like about that very common sort of wrong-doing. But he was not a thief."

"Will you or will you not explain what all this means?" cried Wotton with abrupt annoyance.

"No," replied Gahagan, with a sudden air of relapsing into laziness and fatigue. "Mr. Pond will now oblige."

"Pond wasn't there, was he?" asked Wotton sharply.

"Oh, no," answered Gahagan, rather with the air of one about to go to sleep. "But I can see by his eyebrows that he knows all about it. Besides, it's somebody else's turn."

He closed his eyes with so hopeless a placidity that the baffled Wotton was forced to turn on the third party, rather like a bewildered bull.

"Do you really know anything about this?" he demanded. "What does he mean by saying that the man who hid the ring wasn't a thief?"

"Well, perhaps I can guess a little," said Mr. Pond modestly. "But that's only because I've kept in mind what we said at the beginning—about the misleading way in which real things remind us of romantic things; only they are never rounded off like the romance. You see, the trouble is that, when a real event reminds us of a novel, we unconsciously think we know all about it, because we know all about the novel. We have got into a groove or rut of familiar fiction; and we can't help thinking the groove runs forward and backward as it does in fiction. We've got the whole background of the story at the back of our minds; and we can't believe that we're really in another story. We always assume something that is assumed in the fictional story; and it isn't true. Once assume the wrong beginning, and you'll not only give the wrong answer but you ask the wrong question. In this case, you've got a mystery; but you've got hold of the wrong mystery."

"Gahagan said you would explain everything," said Wotton, with controlled satire. "May I ask if this is the explanation? Is this the solution or the mystery?"

"The real mystery of the ring," said Pond gravely, "is not where it went to, but where it came from."

Wotton stared at him steadily for an instant, and then said in rather a new voice: "Go on."

Mr. Pond went on. "Gahagan has said very truly that poor Pitt-Palmer was not the thief. Pitt-Palmer did not steal the ring."

"Then," exploded Wotton, "who the devil was it who stole the ring?"

"Lord Crome stole the ring," said Mr. Pond.

There was a silence upon the whole group for a brief space; and then the somnolent Gahagan stirred and said: "I knew you would see the point."

By way of making things clearer, Mr. Pond added almost apologetically:

"But, you see, he had to hand it round, to find out whom he had stolen it from."

After a moment he resumed in his usual logical but laborious manner: "Don't you see, as I said, you assume something at the start, simply because it is in all the stories? You assume that when a host hands round something at dinner, it's something belonging to him and his household, probably an old family possession; because that is in all the stories. But Lord Crome meant something much blacker and bitterer than that when he said, with a dreadful irony, that it commemorated a romance in his family.

"Lord Crome had stolen that ring by intercepting correspondence; or, in other words, tearing open an envelope addressed to his wife and containing nothing but the ring. The address was typewritten; nor indeed did he know all the hand-writings involved. But he knew the very ancient writing engraved on that ring; which was such that it could only have been given with one purpose. He assembled those men to find out who was the sender; or, in other words, who was the owner. He knew the owner would somehow attempt to reclaim his possession, if he possibly could; to stop the scandal and remove the evidence. And indeed the man who did so, though he might be a blackguard, would certainly not be a thief. As a matter of fact, after a heathen fashion, he was a bit of a hero. Perhaps it was not for nothing that he had that cold, strong face that is the stone mask of Augustus. He took, first of all, the simple but sensible course of slipping the ring into his black coffee, under cover of a gesture of taking sugar. There it would not be seen, for the moment, anyhow; and he could safely offer himself to be searched. That demented moment, which really seemed to turn the whole thing into a frightful dream, when Crome screamed out that the coffee was poisoned, was only Crome's desperate counter-stroke when he had guessed the trick; to make sure that the coffee should be left alone and the ring recovered. But that young man with the cold face preferred to die in that dreadful fashion: by swallowing the heavy ring and choking; on the chance that his secret, or rather Lady Crome's secret, might yet be overlooked. It was a desperate chance, anyway; but of all the courses open to him, that being his object, it was probably the best he could have taken. In any case, I feel that we must all support Gahagan in saying, very properly, that the poor fellow's memory should be protected from any baser sug-gestions, and that a gentleman is certainly not a robber when he prefers to choke himself with his own ring."

Mr. Pond coughed delicately, having brought his argument to a close; and Sir Hubert Wotton remained staring at him, rather more bewildered by the solution than by the problem. When he rose slowly to his feet, it was with the air of one shaking off something that was still an evil dream, even when he knew that it had happened.

"Well, I've got to be going, anyhow," he said, with an air of heavy relief. "Got to look in at Whitehall and I fancy I'm late already. By the way, if what you say is true, this must have happened very lately. So far as I know, the news of Pitt-Palmer's suicide hasn't come through yet—at least it hadn't come through this morning."

"It happened last night," said Gahagan, and rose from the chair where he had been sprawling, to take leave of his friend.

When Wotton had departed, a long silence fell upon the two other friends who remained looking gravely at each other.

"It happened last night," repeated Gahagan. "That is why I told you it had something to do with what happened this morning. I got engaged to Joan Varney this morning."

"Yes," said Mr. Pond gently. "I think I understand."

"Yes, I think you do," said Gahagan, "but I am going to try to explain, for all that. Do you know there was one thing almost more awful than that poor fellow's death? And it only hit me when I was half a mile from that accursed house. I knew why I had been one of the guests."

He was standing and staring out of the window, with his broad back turned to Pond; and after the last words he was silent and continued to stare at the stormy landscape outside. Perhaps something in it stirred another memory, for when he spoke again, it was as if he started a new subject, though it was another aspect of the same one.

"I didn't tell you anything much about the sort of garden party, with cocktails, that they had that afternoon before the dinner, because I felt that until one realized the climax, one couldn't realize anything; it would all sound like vapouring about the weather. But it was rather rum sort of weather yesterday, as it still is; only it was stormier, and I think the storm has passed over now. And it was a rum sort of atmosphere, too; though the weather was only a coincidence, of course, it does sometimes happen that meteorological conditions make men more conscious of moral conditions. There was a queer, lurid sort of sky over the garden, though there was a fair amount of fitful sunshine almost as capricious as lightning. A huge great mountain of cloud, coloured like ink and indigo, was coming up behind the pale, pillared façade of the house, which was still in a wan flush of light; and I remember even then being chilled by a childish fancy that Pitt-Palmer was a pale marble statue and part of the building. But there was little else to give any hint of the secret; nobody could say that Lady Crome was like a statue; for she went flying and flaunting about like a bird of paradise. But, whether you believe it or not, I did from the first feel an oppression, both physical and psychical; especially psychical. It increased when we went indoors and the dining-room curtains cut us off from any actual sight of the storm. They were old-fashioned, dark-red curtains, with heavy, gilded tassels; and it was as if everything was steeped in the same dye. You've heard of a man seeing red; well, what I saw was dark red. That's as near as I can get to the feeling; for it was a feeling from the first; and I guessed nothing.

"And then that sinister and revolting thing happened before my eyes at the table; I can see the dark red wine in the port decanters and the dull glow of the lampshades. And still it seemed as if I were invisible and impersonal; I was hardly conscious of myself. Of course, we all had to answer some questions about ourselves; but I need not tell you about the trail of official fussing that crossed the track of the tragedy. It did not take long, since it was so obviously a case of suicide;

and the party broke up, straggling out into the stormy night through the garden. As they passed out, they seemed to have taken on new shapes, new outlines. Between the hot night and the horrible death and that foul fog of throttling hatred in which we had tried to breathe, I began to see something else about them; perhaps to see them as they were. They were no longer incongruous but grotesquely congruous; as in a hideous *camaraderie*. Of course, this was a mood, and a morbid one; they really had been different enough; but they had something in common.

"I liked the Pole best; he had a sense of humour, and admirable manners; but I knew what he meant when he so courteously declined the position of Pope, because it would involve celibacy. Crome knew it too, and grinned back at him like a demon. The other one I liked was Major Wooster, the Anglo-Indian; but something told me that he was really of the jungle; a *shikar* not only hunting tigers, a tiger not only hunting deer. Then there was the titled doctor with the Assyrian brows and beard; I bet he was more Semitic than Magyar. But anyhow, he had thick lips in his thick beard, and a look in his almond eyes that I did not like at all. One of the worst of them, I should say. I wouldn't say anything worse of Blande than that he's probably too stupid to understand anything but his own body. He hasn't enough mind to know that he has a mind. We all know Sir Oscar Marvell; I remember him marching out, his furred cloak flapping as if it trailed behind it infinite echoes of the harmless applause of flappers—but of more foolish women as well. As to the Italian tenor, he was uncommonly like the English actor. One could not say any worse of him than that.

"Yes; they were, after all, a very select company. They were selected by a clever if nearly crazy man as being the six men in London most likely to lay a plot to seduce his wife. Then, with a great shock, I quite literally came to myself. I actually realized my own presence. I was there, too. Crome had made up a choice party of profligates and picked them carefully. And he had honoured *me* with an invitation to the feast.

"That was what I was. That, at least, was what I was supposed to be. A damned dandy and dawdling blackguard, always dangling after other men's wives. . . . You know, Pond, that I was not really so bad as all that; but then, perhaps, neither were they. We were all innocent in this case; and yet the thundercloud upon the garden rested on us like a judgment. So was I innocent, in that case you remember, when I nearly got hanged for hanging round a woman I really didn't care about. But it served us right; it was our atmosphere that was all wrong—what quaint old people used to call the state of our souls, what the unspeakable bounders in the papers call sex-appeal. That was why I nearly got hanged; and why there was a corpse in the house behind me. And there went through my head like the tramp of armies, old lines written long ago, about what is in legend the noblest of all lawless loves, when Guinevere, refusing Lancelot at the last, says in words that had for me a ring of iron:

> "For well ye wot that of this life
> There comes but lewd and bitter strife
> And death of men and great travail.

"I had hung round all that sort of thing, and yet never quite clearly seen myself doing it; till two judgments struck me like the storm out of the sky. I nearly received a sentence from a judge in a black cap and blood-red robes, that I should be hanged by the neck until I was dead. And, worse still, I received an invitation from Lord Crome."

He continued to gaze out of the window; but Pond heard him mutter again, like the faint grumbling of the thunder: "*And death of men and great travail.*"

In the vast silence that followed, Mr. Pond said in a very small voice:

"What was the matter with you was that you liked being libelled."

Gahagan faced about, almost with the gesture of throwing up his hands, which seemed to fill the frame of the window with his own gigantic frame; but he was noticeably pale.

"*Kamerad,* yes," he said. "I was as small as that."

He smiled at his friend, but with a glassy and rather ghastly smile, and then went on:

"Yes; I cared more for that dirty rag of vanity, worse than any vice, than I did for any vices. How many men have sold their souls to be admired by fools? I nearly did it, merely to be suspected by fools. To be the dangerous man, the dark horse, the man of whom families should be afraid—that is the sort of abject ambition for which I wasted so much of my life, and nearly lost the fulfilment of my love. I dawdled, I lounged about, because I could not give up a bad name. And, by God, it nearly hanged the dog."

"That is what I supposed," said Mr. Pond in his most prime and polite manner. And then Gahagan broke out again:

"I was better than I seemed. But what did that mean, except the spiritual blasphemy that I wanted to seem worse than I was? What could it mean, except that, far worse than one who practised vice, I admired it? Yes, admired it in myself; even when it wasn't there. I was the new hypocrite; but mine was the homage that virtue pays to vice."

"I understand, however," said Mr. Pond, in that curiously cold and distant tone, which had yet a very soothing effect on everybody, "that you are now effectually cured."

"I am cured," said Gahagan grimly. "But it took two dead men and a gallows to cure me. But the point is, what was I cured of? You have diagnosed it exactly right, my dear doctor, if I may call you so. I could not give up the secret pleasure of being slandered."

"By this time, however," said Mr. Pond, "other considerations have come in and induced you to support the insupportable charge of virtue."

Gahagan suddenly laughed, harshly and yet, somehow, heartily. Some would count his first comment a peculiar extension of the laugh. "I went to confession and the rest of it this morning," he said, "and in a vaguer sort of way I've come to confession to you. To confess that I didn't kill the man. To confess that I never made love to the man's wife. In short, to confess that I was a humbug. To confess that I am not a dangerous man . . . well, anyhow, after I'd done all that, I went on whistling, and as happy as a bird, to—well, I think you know where I went to. There's a girl I ought to have fixed things up with long ago; and I always wanted to do it; that's the paradox. But a damned sight sillier paradox than any of your paradoxes, Pond."

Mr. Pond laughed gently, as he generally did when somebody had told him, at considerable length, all that he knew already. And he was not so old, nor despite his manner so cold, as not to form some sort of guess about the actual termination of the rather exasperating romance of Captain Gahagan.

This story started with some statements about the way in which stories tend to get into a tangle, one tale being mixed up with another tale, especially when they are true tales. This story also started, and ought also presumably to stop, with the very extraordinary tragedy and scandal in the house of Lord Crome, when that promising young politician, Mr. Pitt-Palmer, unaccountably tumbled down dead. It ought really to end with a proper account of his impressive public funeral; of the chorus of praise devoted to him in the Press; and the stately compliments laid on his tomb like flowers from the leaders of all the parties in Parliament; from those eloquent words of the Leader of the Opposition beginning "Much as we may have differed in politics," to those (if possible) still more eloquent observations of the Leader of the House, beginning "Confident as I am that our cause is independent even of the noblest personality, I yet have to lament, etc."

Anyhow, it is really very irrelevant to the central plot of this story that it should stray from the funeral of Pitt-Palmer to the wedding of Gahagan. It will be enough to say that, as already hinted, the actual effect of this shocking incident on Gahagan was to drive him back to an old love; an old love who was still conveniently young. A certain Miss Violet Varney was at that time prominent on the stage; the word "prominent" has been selected with some care from other possible adjectives. In the general view of society, Miss Joan Varney was the sister of Miss Violet Varney. In the perverse and personal view of Captain Gahagan, Miss Violet Varney was the sister of Miss Joan Varney; nor was he eager to insist on this relationship. He loved Joan but he did not even like Violet; but there is no need to enter on the entanglements of that other story here. Are not all these things written in the Chronicles of the Kings of Israel?

It is enough to say that on that particular morning, swept clear and shining after the storm, Captain Gahagan came out of the church in the little by-street and very cheerfully took the road to the house of the Varney family, where he found Miss Joan Varney pottering about in the garden with a spud, and told her several things of some importance to both of them. When Miss Violet Varney heard that her younger sister was engaged to Captain Gahagan, she went off with admirable promptitude to a theatrical club and got engaged to one of the numerous noodles of more or less noble birth who could be used for the purpose. She very sensibly broke off this engagement about a month afterwards; but she got *her* engagement into the society papers first.

The Terrible Troubadour

"IN NATURE you must go very low to find things that go so high." This was commonly included by collectors among the Paradoxes of Mr. Pond; for it came towards the end of a rather dull and eminently sensible discourse, and it made no sense. And these were recognized as the stigmata of the stylistic methods of Mr. Pond. But in this case, as a fact, he had plagiarized from his old acquaintance Dr. Paul Green, author of *The Dog or the Monkey*, *Studies in the Domestication of Anthropoids*, *Notes on Neanderthal Development*, etc., etc.

Dr. Paul Green was a smallish man, pale, slender and slightly lame; but his activity, even in bodily movement, was relatively remarkable, and his mind moved as quickly as a quick-firing gun.

It was this old acquaintance who, on one sunny afternoon, came out of Mr. Pond's past to bring him shocking and even nerve-shattering news; a report as alarming as the report of a gun.

But when Mr. Pond was told, on such very solid authority, that his friend Captain Gahagan was an escaped murderer, after all, he said, "Tut, tut." He was given to what is called understatement; of which he knew the Greek name, but did not employ it needlessly. The conversation, indeed, had opened casually enough, turning from the doctor's health to the doctor's hobby of studying animal habits. A little light talk about Eohippus; some airy badinage about Homo Kanensis; a little bright back-chat about Vialleton's *Études sur les Réflexes des Animaux Tétrapodes;* rising to a certain sharpness of dialogue, for on this point of Darwin and Natural Selection the two friends had never agreed.

"I never can see," said Mr. Pond, "how a change, that might have helped an animal if it came quickly, could have helped him if it came slowly. And came to his great-grandchild, long after he ought to have perished without leaving any grandchildren. It might be better if I had three legs, say, in order to stand firmly on two while kicking a fellow bureaucrat with the third. It might be better if I had three legs; but it wouldn't be better if I only had a rudimentary leg."

"It might be better if I had two legs," said the doctor grimly, "instead of one lame leg that is hardly a leg at all. And yet I find it fairly useful."

Mr. Pond, who was commonly very tactful, chid himself softly for tactlessness in forgetting that his old acquaintance was lame. But, at least, he was far too tactful to apologize, or even too obviously to change the subject.

He proceeded in his mild and fluent way: "I mean that till a leg is long enough to run or climb, it would only be an extra weight for the runner or climber to carry."

"It's pretty queer," said the doctor, "that we should have started off talking about running and climbing. I didn't come here to discuss Darwinism or anything half so sane and sensible. But if you think I'm suspect, as the atrocious atheist, I may explain that I don't want you just now to listen to me, but to my friend the vicar of Hanging Burgess, the Reverend Cyprian Whiteways, whose views are probably quite as anti-scientific as your own. I don't suppose he's a Darwinian; but, anyhow, I promised to introduce him to you, and he wants to tell you about things that happened rather later than the later Stone Age."

"Then, what do you mean," asked Pond, "by talking about running and climbing?"

"I meant, I am sorry to say," replied Dr. Green, "that the vicar has a pretty bad story about that friend of yours, Captain Gahagan, whose legs seem to be very good at climbing, and still better at running away."

"It's a serious thing," said Pond, gravely, "to accuse a soldier of running away."

"It's a much more serious thing of which the vicar accuses him," said Green. "He accuses him of climbing a balcony and shooting a rival, and then running away. But it's not my story; I'm not the story, but only the introduction."

"Climbing a balcony," mused Mr. Pond; "for a vicar it sounds rather a romantic story."

"I know," said the doctor, "the sort of story that begins with a rope-ladder and ends with a rope."

Mr. Pond, as he heard the unequal step of his lame friend echoing away down the paved paths of the garden, relapsed into a gloomy mood. He was quite willing to accept his medical friend merely as a letter of introduction. But it was a rather black-edged and tragic sort of letter of introduction. Whatever story the Rev. Cyprian was going to tell, it was another story against his unfortunate friend Peter Gahagan. And Gahagan was so very unfortunate as to suggest to some a wild doubt about whether he was merely unfortunate. Some had the sudden and horrible thought that, perhaps, he was fortunate. Twice before, he had been mixed up in matters involving a mysterious and violent death; with, at least, a savour of murder. In both cases he had been cleared. But three is an unlucky number.

Finally, the Rev. Cyprian Whiteways was a shock; a shock because of his frankness and fair-mindedness.

Mr. Pond would never, at any time, have stooped to the stupid idea that clergymen are stupid. He did not take his ideas of real life from farces like *The Private Secretary*. But the Rev. Cyprian was so very much the reverse of stupid; a man with a rugged face like old red sandstone; and, indeed, he suggested a rock of that rich colouring which glows with the past; he carried his English countryside with him in an indescribable suggestion of depth and background; he could not talk of common things without, somehow, suggesting the weather or the turn of night or day; he was a born descriptive writer who only talked. But nobody could doubt that it was truth; or, at least, truthfulness.

It was so substantial a witness who told Mr. Pond in considerable detail the black and bloody story of Gahagan's hidden sin. And the curious effect of all this on Mr. Pond was to make him jump up briskly with a broad smile of relief on his bearded and somewhat owlish visage; declaring with unusual cheeriness that it was quite all right, they had only to ask Gahagan himself, and he would tell them all about it. Confrontation, it was sometimes called.

As for Dr. Green, with the letter of introduction, his job was done, and he was somewhat impatient of Pond's formalities; he stumped off, merely warning the vicar that he had better have a lawyer, if he was to confront that plausible Irish rogue.

So, when the scientist was already far away, reabsorbed in the study of a pithecanthropos as a pet, all that remained of his intervention was a solicitor named Luke Little, very much on the spot.

Mr. Pond's friend, Sir Hubert Wotton, the well-known diplomatist, took the chair; but Mr. Little did not mind who took chairs so long as he took charge.

"This is a very irregular inquiry, gentlemen," he said. "Only a special assurance would have induced me to place my client's case before it. Sir Hubert and Mr. Pond declare, I understand, that an explanation will be demanded here and now."

Then he added: "It is a painful matter, as I think Mr. Pond will agree."

"It is a very painful matter, indeed," replied Pond, gravely, "that an old friend of mine should be under suspicion of a horrible action."

His friend, Wotton, looked at Pond for a moment with a frosty stare of surprise; but he stared a great deal more when he was startled by Gahagan himself, speaking, suddenly, for the first and last time in all the first hours of the interview.

"Yes," he said, with a grim and inscrutable visage. "It is certainly a horrible story."

"In any case, then," resumed the lawyer, "I can now ask my client, without prejudice, to repeat the story."

"It's an ugly story," said the clergyman in his honest way, "and I'll tell it as shortly as I can."

Pond had heard the story, already, told in a way at once looser and more elaborate, and allowing of more descriptive detail or inference than the statement made under such very legal supervision. But even as he heard it again in more exact form, he could not get rid of a feeling that the scene described was unnaturally vivid to him, but with the vividness of a nightmare.

There was no particular reason, at that stage, for comparing the story to a nightmare; except that the two principal incidents happened at night.

They happened in the vicar's garden, close to the balcony of the vicar's house; and perhaps the impression, which was rather like an oppression, was somehow connected with another night darkening the night; a living night of vegetation; for it was suggested, throughout, that the balcony was loaded with pots and palms and clutched by climbing plants with heavy and pendent leaves.

Perhaps, after all, it was only some vague, verbal association with the name of Hanging Burgess; as if the mystery were somehow associated with the hanging gardens of Babylon. Perhaps, again, it was partly the irrational trail of the talk with Dr. Green, with his creed of blind growth and a groping life-force in a godless dark; for Green developed his view of development with every fancy from botany as well as biology.

On the whole, however, Mr. Pond concluded that his own queer mood was the result of the one fact, which it had really been necessary to describe in detail. For the vicar had been obliged to explain, on both occasions, in order to make his tale intelligible, that the front of the balcony was scaled from below by a titanic, tropical creeper, with ribbed and interlaced limbs and large, fantastic leaves. It is not altogether an exaggeration to say that the creeper was the principal character in the story.

"This business happened during the Great War," explained the clergyman, "when my daughter and I were living in my house at Hanging Burgess. But the two houses on each side of us were empty, due to the drainage of human material common at the time. At least, they were both empty for a considerable period, though they were handsome houses with large gardens, sloping down to the river. Then my friend Dr. Green came down to be my next-door neighbour and prosecute his scientific researches in a quiet place. He was writing a book, you know, on the domestication of animals; dogs and cats and pet marmosets and monkeys, and so on; and my daughter, who is interested in such pets, helped him a little with his work.

"It is a happy time to look back upon, for us who were old cronies; perhaps because it was a quiet time.

"And then our solitude was broken, as it seemed by accident, and all the trouble and tragedy began.

"First of all, a young artist of the name of Albert Ayres rented the house next door, though he seemed to want it mostly for a base in which to leave his baggage, for he was wandering over the country making sketches; and it is only fair, as you will see presently, to admit that he did say, once, that he would start straight away next morning on one of his sketching tours. I mean that we cannot, in any case, actually prove what became of him. Unfortunately, I know only too well what became of him.

"He was an interesting individual; perhaps a little too like the old notion of an artist; the sort one can hardly call either carelessly or carefully picturesque; with a halo of yellow hair which the sympathetic might connect with Galahad and the unsympathetic with Struwwelpeter. Mind you, there was nothing about him effeminate, and nothing false about his position in relation to the war. He had been invalided out, and what he was doing was a necessary job and not a funk-hole; and, at the moment, he was enjoying a short and very well-earned holiday.

"It is only fair to Captain Gahagan to say that, even in their subsequent quarrel, even in the last, blackest days of hatred, and, I hope, of madness, which ended in murder, the Captain never sneered at his rival upon that point, or assumed anything like the swagger of khaki. But, at the time, Captain Gahagan was still in khaki, having a very short leave from the front, which he was supposed to spend at the neighbouring inn, but did spend mostly in my house.

"You will understand my reluctance in speaking of the matter; the fact that he was on short leave may have given a certain impatience to his rather headlong courtship of my daughter, for it could be called nothing else. Some say that women do not specially object to that; but I would much prefer not to presume on any speculations about that matter. But to deal entirely with the facts. They are as follows:

"One evening, just after sunset, or about dusk, I was walking in my garden with the doctor, and we were joined, shortly afterwards, by Albert Ayres. I had just asked my friend Green to drop in and take some dinner with us; but he happened to be rather exhausted with a heavy day of his scientific work; he looked pale and tired; and he declined in a rather distant and distracted manner. In fact, I thought he was looking ill."

"He has not very good health," interposed Mr. Pond, suddenly. "He doesn't go about very much. You must remember he is lame."

The others stared at him again, as if not seeing any importance in the interruption; and again they were still more puzzled by his further comment; for he added quite calmly:

"The clue to all this mystery is the fact that Dr. Green is lame."

"I have not the wildest notion what you mean," said the vicar of Hanging Burgess briskly. "But, anyhow, I had better get on and tell you what really happened; and you will see that it certainly had nothing to do with either lameness or Dr. Green.

"In strolling round the garden we had paused under the giant creeper that grows out of the flower-bed and shoots right up to the balcony; and Ayres was just remarking on its unique strength and luxuriousness, when we all had a sort of a shock. For we saw the whole creeper move and twist like a monstrous serpent, in that still garden; every limb of it heaved and writhed and the whole framework of its foliage was shaken as by some impossibly localized earthquake.

Then we saw that long legs like a giant's were swinging downwards and kicking wildly above our heads; and Captain Gahagan, missing his last foothold, fell on his feet on the gravel path and faced us with a broad grin.

"'Pray forgive me,' he said, 'I have been paying an afternoon call. I dropped in to tea, or perhaps I should say, hopped up to tea; and I have just dropped out again.'

"I told him, perhaps a little frigidly, that we were always pleased to receive visitors, but that they generally came in by the front door. He asked me, in a rather brazen way, if I had no poetic sympathy with Romeo and the romance of climbing balconies. I preferred not to reply; but my friend, the doctor, was staring curiously at the creeper, probably in some freak of his merely botanical curiosity; and he said, with his faintly acid humour: 'Isn't there rather a satire on Romeo in the fact that a weed like that can climb a balcony? It isn't quite so common to see a tropical plant ringing the bell and coming in at the front door. Climbing doesn't seem a safe way of classifying. In nature, you must go very low to find things that go so high.'"

Mr. Pond sat up abruptly and seemed to exhale a breath; but all he said was, "I thought so."

"The artist named Ayres," continued the vicar, "seemed more annoyed than either of us at this absurd adventure; and his comment was really much more provocative, though he only said, coolly: 'Well, it looks an easy thing to climb; as easy as a great, green ladder. I fancy I could climb it myself, if it came to that.'

"Then I realized for the first time, for I'm rather slow in these things, that Gahagan was glaring at him, as he answered sharply: 'Am I to understand that it may come to that?' And then I realized that they were both glaring at each other; and I guessed, for the first time, why they hated each other; and what was the meaning of that scene in my quiet garden.

"Well, I will get on as quickly as I can to the culmination of these rash boasts, or challenges, of the two tragic rivals. For, indeed, I do not know which of them had the worst tragedy. Night had fallen and the moon had risen, though it was not very much later, cutting up the shady garden into a new pattern of shadows, when I happened to look out of my study window, which is on an upper floor.

"I was smoking and reading a book, when a noise like a dog barking, or rather howling, made me put my head, more or less carelessly, out of the window; I assumed that it was one of Dr. Green's dogs and did not think much of the matter; subconsciously, perhaps, something spectral about the moonstruck garden and the mood that it stirred, or some more mysterious premonition of what was to follow, made the howl sound more hollow and even horrible than it really was.

"A clear moon was rising high behind me; most of the shady garden was in all the denser shade; but there were large, pale patches and squares of moonshine on the paths and the wall in front of me, cut out as sharply as the pasteboard frame of some shadow-pantomime. Perhaps the parallel seized on my fancy, partly because light and shadow were thus bent or doubled into different planes, vertical or horizontal, like the black and white paper from which children cut out the figures for such a play. Anyhow, I did think, instantly and very vividly, of a shadow-pantomime; and, the next instant, I saw one of the pantomime figures passing in black silhouette across the wall.

"I knew at once whose shadow it was. Of course, it was drawn out and distorted; you know how deceptive shadows are; but I could see the straggling tufts that reminded one of Struwwelpeter; and I think I told you before that Ayres, the artist, was a little too like the traditional artist who hasn't had his hair cut. Also, he affected that sort of languid stoop that such artists assume; and there was the high-shouldered stoop exaggerated, as shadows do exaggerate.

"The next moment, another of these dark caricatures had appeared on the wall; and it was even more unmistakable. It was also more active; it was not only a shadow-pantomime but—in a pretty creepy sense—a knockabout pantomime."

"Shadows are very deceptive," said Mr. Pond; and again his friends stared at him, not because his intervention was important, but because it seemed trivial and totally unnecessary. But before he relapsed again into silence, he added:

"The most deceptive thing about a shadow is that it may be quite accurate."

"Well, really!" exploded Wotton; but his moderately mild explosion was overshadowed by one of the abrupt movements which once or twice moved the gigantic Gahagan to overwhelming but rather baffling gestures, to detached and yet outrageous interventions. He turned to his accuser with a bow of overbearing courtesy, or even courtliness, and said:

"You need not be alarmed, sir. That is one of Mr. Pond's paradoxes. We are all very proud of our Pond and of his paradoxes. Try them in your bath. Pond's paradoxes are in every home. What would Mother do without Pond's——"

"Don't be a fool, Gahagan!" said Hubert Wotton; and his voice had a ring of steel which his friends had always respected. There was a silence, in which Mr. Pond said simply:

"I never uttered a paradox in my life. What I said was a truism."

The vicar of Hanging Burgess looked considerably baffled, but did not lose his composure, and continued his story.

"I'm afraid all this seems to me rather off the point; especially as I haven't come to the point. I mean the point of my story. Of course, it doesn't matter whether the shadows were deceptive or not; because I saw the real people a minute or two afterwards. It's true I only saw one of them for a minute, you might say for a flash; but the other I saw plainly enough.

"The first figure, the long-haired figure I had already identified with the artist, ran very quickly across the moonlit patch and vanished into the vast shadow of the creeper that climbed the balcony; but there is no doubt that he began to climb the creeper.

"The second figure stood for a moment, staring, in the full stare of the moon; and there was no doubt about him at all. It was Captain Gahagan, in khaki, and he already had his big service revolver in his hand. In a high, unnatural voice he cried after and cursed the other unfortunate troubadour, who had climbed his romantic rope-ladder of leaves, exactly as he had climbed it himself.

"At that instant the whole situation became finally clear; for I saw the hairy head of the unfortunate artist rising out of the tangle of tropical leaves, in shadow, but all the more unmistakable for being haloed in the moonshine. But the same moonshine fell full on the face of the Captain, as glaring as a photographic portrait; and it glared with a frightful grin or grimace of hatred."

Mr. Pond again interposed gently, but with the general effect of a jerk: "You say it was hatred. Are you sure it was not horror?"

The vicar was very intelligent, and thought before he answered, even when he did not in the least understand. Then he said: "I think so. Besides, why should Captain Gahagan be horrified merely at seeing Mr. Ayres?"

"Perhaps," said Pond, after a pause, "because he had not had his hair cut."

"Pond!" said Wotton very sharply. "Do you fancy this is a case for jokes? You seem to have forgotten that you said, yourself, it was a painful matter."

"I said it was a painful matter," said Pond, "to think a horrible thing was done by an old friend." Then he said, after one of his sudden pauses: "But I wasn't thinking of Gahagan."

The stupefied vicar seemed to have given up everything but the stubborn pursuit of his story.

"As I have told you, Captain Gahagan cursed his rival from below, and called on him to come down; but he did not attempt to climb the creeper himself, though he had already shown how quickly he could do it. Unfortunately, he did something else; which he could do much more quickly. I saw the blue flash of the pistol-barrel in the moon, as he lifted it; and then the red flash; and then a puff of smoke detached itself and climbed the sky, like a cloud; and the man on the green ladder fell crashing like a stone through the thrashing great leaves to the dark space below.

"I could not see so clearly what was happening in that dark space; but I knew, for all practical purposes, that the man was dead; for his slayer laid hold of one leg of the corpse and dragged it away down the darkling and descending paths of the garden. And when I heard a distant splash, I knew he had thrown the corpse into the river.

"Well, as I told you before, that is my very serious testimony to what I saw and knew; but I give it only from a sense of social duty to any individuals who may be involved; I admit the circumstances are such that legal proof would be very difficult now.

"Albert Ayres had entirely disappeared by next morning; but it is true, as I have said, that he had once spoken of going off on a sketching-tour very early.

"Captain Gahagan had also entirely disappeared by next morning; but I believe it is true that his leave was practically up, that in any case he had to return to the front; and it was utterly hopeless to raise a question—which would, already, be called a doubtful question—at a moment when every man was needed, when common convicts were already working out their expiation in the field; and when all information had to be hampered, and a veil hung between us and all that vast labyrinth called 'somewhere in France.' But hearing that, for personal reasons, it was essential that Captain Gahagan should be asked to clear or explain his record, I have brought the matter up again now. And I have stated nothing that I did not see."

"You have stated it very clearly," said Mr. Pond. "More clearly than you know. But even on the clearest moonlight night, as we agreed, shadows can be very deceptive."

"You've said that before," said Sir Hubert rather irritably.

"And, as I have also said before," observed the unruffled Mr. Pond, "a shadow is most misleading when it is precisely correct."

Silence suddenly fell on the group; and the silence became more and more tense, for, after these random shots, which seemed so very random, fired by Mr. Pond as he retired from the argument, everyone felt that nothing could now delay the main action. For some time it looked rather like inaction; for Gahagan, who had been growing gloomier and gloomier, still sat kicking his heels, as if he had nothing to say. And indeed, when sharply called on by Sir Hubert for his statement, he was, at first, understood to declare seriously, not to say grimly, that he had nothing to say.

"What can I say, except what they call pleading guilty? What can I say, except that I did do a horrible thing; I did commit a hateful crime; and my sin is ever before me."

The solicitor seemed suddenly to bristle with electric needles of a sort of cold excitement.

"Pardon me, pardon me!" he cried. "Before you say any more, before you say a word more, it must be understood that it may be necessary to take note of it in a legal manner. On some minor matters we are permitted a certain discretion; but if we are to listen to an actual confession of murder——"

Gahagan shouted; he shouted so loud that the others were almost too surprised to notice that it was a shout of laughter, but not very genial laughter.

"What!" he cried. "Do you think I'm confessing to a murder? Oh, this is getting tiresome! Of course I never committed any murder. I said I committed a crime; but it's not to any damned little lawyer that I have to apologize for it."

He swung round, facing the clergyman; and his whole bodily and mental attitude seemed to alter; so that, when he spoke at last, it was like a new man speaking.

"I mean, it's for you. What can I say to you? It's personal for you; I mean, it's real. It's no good talking at large about such things. It's no good hiding in a crowd; or saying that the crime was committed by a lot of poor devils on leave from hell; to whom a holiday was heaven; only it was a very earthly paradise; a little too like a Moslem paradise. I did make love to your daughter when I had no right to, for I didn't really know my own mind. None of us had any mind on those holidays from hell. And it's true that I did have a rival. It's true I was in a rage with my rival; I'm still in a rage with him, when I think of what he did. Only——" He paused, as with a new embarrassment.

"Go on," said Mr. Pond, gently.

"Only my rival wasn't the artist with the long hair," said Gahagan.

Hubert Wotton again looked up sharply, with a frowning stare; but he spoke quietly as he directed Gahagan to tell his story properly from the start.

"I had better start," said Gahagan, "where the other story started: just about the time when we both heard the howl of a dog in the dark garden. I may explain that I was actually staying with Ayres, the artist, for that night; we had become quite good friends, really; though there may have been a bit of romantic swagger about the troubadour business at an earlier time.

"I was packing up and sorting out some of my light luggage; that is how I happened to be cleaning my service revolver. Ayres was looking through some of his sketch-books; and I left him at it when I went out, just as Mr. Whiteways looked out, in casual curiosity, over that sudden noise in the night. Only I heard what he did not hear. I not only heard what sounded like the howl of a dog, but I also heard a whistle, such as a man uses when calling a dog.

"Also, I saw what he did not see. For an instant, in a gap in the trellis and tracery of a vine, I saw, very white in the moonlight, the face of Paul Green, that distinguished man of science. He is distinguished and he looks distinguished; I remember thinking, at the time, what a fine head he had, and that the silver moulding of his features under the moon made them quite beautiful. I had a reason for having my attention thus arrested by that silvery mask, for, at that precise moment, it wore a sort of smile of hatred that turned one's blood cold.

"Then the face vanished; and again my experience was much like the vicar's, except that I did not see everything which happened just behind my back. But I swung round in time to see that somebody had run across the path, and begun to climb the creeper. He climbed it very quickly, much quicker than I had done, but it was not easy to see him or recognize him in the dark shadow of the leaves.

"I had an idea that he was long in the limbs and had the sort of high-shouldered stoop that has been described; then I saw, as the vicar did, the head emerge clear of the foliage, only outlined by the moon with a sort of bristly halo of hair. Only then, for the second time that night, I saw what the vicar did not see. The Romeo, the climbing troubadour, turned his head, and, for a moment, I saw it in profile, a black shape against the moon. And I said to myself: 'My God! It's a dog, after all.' "

The vicar echoed the invocation faintly; the lawyer made a sharp movement as if to intervene; and Wotton told his friend rather brusquely to go on; which had the effect of producing a sort of abrupt languor, alarmingly like a disposition to leave off.

"Rather interesting man, Marco Polo," said Captain Gahagan, in a vaguely conversational tone. "I think it was Marco Polo, the Venetian; anyhow, it was one of those early mediæval travellers. You know everybody used to say they told nothing but tall stories about mandrakes and mermaids; but, in many cases, it has been found since that their tall tales were true. Anyhow, this chap said there were men walking about with the heads of dogs. Now, if you'll look at one of the larger apes, like the baboon, you'll see that his head really is very like a dog's; not nearly so much like a man's as the head of one of the smaller monkeys."

Mr. Little, the lawyer, was rapidly turning over some of his papers, with a shrewd frown and a sharp, alert manner.

"One moment, Captain Gahagan," he interposed. "I have a fancy that you are rather a traveller, yourself; and have picked up travellers' tales in many different places. It looks to me as if you had picked up this one in the *Rue Morgue*."

"I wish I had," replied the Captain.

"In the story there," pursued the solicitor, "I think there was an escaped anthropoid ape who disobeyed his master and would not return."

"Yes," said Mr. Pond, in a low voice, rather like a groan. "But in this case it was not disobeying its master."

"You had better tell the rest of this story, Pond," said the Captain, with one of his curious collapses into irresponsible repose. "You evidently guessed the real story, I don't know how, before I began to tell it."

Mr. Little appeared to be somewhat annoyed, and snapped out: "I consider the Captain told this curious tale, for what it is worth, in a very melodramatic and misleading manner. I have it, in my notes, that he certainly said that 'Somebody ran across the path and began to climb the creeper.'"

"I was quite pedantically correct," said Gahagan, waving his hand, condescendingly. "I was careful to state that some *body* ran and climbed. I attempted no theological or metaphysical speculations about the soul of an ape."

"But this is perfectly ghastly!" cried the clergyman, who was deeply shaken. "Are you sure the thing I saw was an ape?"

"I was quite close," said the Captain. "I saw the shape and you only saw the shadow."

"No," said Pond softly, "he saw the shape and could not believe it because it was the shadow. That is what I meant by saying a shadow can deceive by accuracy. Nine times out of ten, a shadow is out of drawing. But it can happen, in special circumstances, that it is an exact silhouette. Only we always expect it to be distorted; and so we are deceived by its not being distorted. The vicar was not surprised that the hairy, high-shouldered Mr. Ayres should throw a shadow looking like a shambling hunchback or a bristly, humped figure. But in reality it *was* a bristly, humped figure. I guessed that when he first said, just afterwards, that your own figure was much more unmistakable. Why should it be unmistakable, unless the other was a mistake?"

"From where I was, there could be no mistake," said Gahagan. "I knew it was an ape, and I guessed it was from the cages or kennels of the eminent biologist next door. I had a wild hope it might have been meant as some ghastly joke; but I wasn't taking any risks; I happen to know that sort of anthropoid is no joke. At the best, he might easily bite and then—well, there were all sorts of nightmare notions half-formed in one's mind.

"There was another side to your biological friend's interest in pets; vivisection, inoculation, intoxication, drugs—Lord knows what might be mixed up in it. So I shot the brute dead, and I'm afraid I can't apologize. I threw the body into the river; as you know, it's a very rapid and rushing river, and, so far as I know, nothing more was ever heard of it. Certainly, Dr. Paul Green did not venture to advertise for it in the papers."

The solid and deep-chested rustic parson suddenly shuddered from head to foot. The spasm passed and he said, heavily, that it was an awful business.

"And *that* is what I meant," said Mr. Pond, "by saying how bad it is to hear an old acquaintance accused of a horrible action. It was, also, what I meant by saying that the key to all this riddle is the fact that Dr. Green is lame."

"Even now," muttered the vicar, "I'm not so clear what you mean by that."

"It's all ugly enough," answered Pond, "but I suppose we may fairly say that the doctor is, in a rather literal sense, a mad doctor. The point is that I think I know what finally drove him mad. He had a remarkable personality; he was in love with the lady at the Vicarage and had got a good deal of influence there; as Gahagan truly says, he's really a very fine-looking fellow and, naturally, quite active; only everything was conditioned by the accident that he was lame.

"What put the finishing touch to his madness, on that terrible summer night under the moon, was something that I think one can partly understand, with a little imagination; something not altogether unnatural, if anything ending in such insanity can be anything but unnatural. He heard his rivals boasting about doing the one thing he could not do. First, one of the young men swaggered about having done it—you do swagger, Gahagan, and it's no good saying you don't. And the other young man was worse; for he actually sneered at doing it because it was so easy to do when, for Green, it was impossible to do.

"Naturally, a mind like his leapt, as we know it did leap, even in conversation, to the retort that climbing is no great sign of superiority; that a brainless creeper can climb; that an ape can climb better than a man. 'You have to go very low to find things that go so high.' Considered as a logical repartee, it was quite a good one. But his mind was not running merely on logic and repartee; he was blind and boiling with jealousy and passion, and he was a little cracked. Let's hope he only meant to make a sort of demonstration; but, anyhow, that was what he was trying to demonstrate."

Mr. Little, the lawyer, still turned a flinty face to the company; he had obviously taken a dislike to Gahagan, who had a way of irritating legal and law-abiding persons.

"I do not know if we are required to accept this extraordinary story, on the strength of Mr. Pond's ingenious hypothesis," he said rather sharply; "but there is one more question I should like to ask."

He looked down at his papers, as if consulting them, and then looked up again, saying, still more sharply, in the style he had learnt from cross-examinations: "Is it not true, Captain Gahagan, that you are rather famous for telling remarkable stories? I have it in my notes that you once delighted the company by saying you had seen six great sea-serpents, each swallowing the last. You reported a remarkable little incident of a giant who was buried up to the eyebrows in Muswell Hill; and you are supposed to have given a very vivid description of a water-spout frozen all the way up to the sky. Your interesting account of the discovery of the ruins of the Tower of Babel——"

Sir Hubert Wotton, with all his apparent simplicity, had a quality of sense that sometimes struck like a sledge-hammer. He had preserved the silence of perfect impartiality throughout; but he suddenly stopped the last splutter of the solicitor's spitefulness, as if he had struck him physically dumb.

"I cannot have all this," he said. "We know Gahagan; and his yarns are all nonsense, and your trying to turn them against him is worse nonsense. So long as you had a serious charge to bring, we gave you every opportunity to prove it. If you are going to talk about things that nobody alive ever took seriously, least of all Gahagan, I rule them out.''

''Very well,'' snapped Mr. Little, ''my last question shall be a very practical one. If Captain Gahagan only did what he says he did, why the devil didn't he say so? Why did he disappear? Why did he do a bolt early next morning?''

Peter Gahagan lifted his large figure laboriously out of the seat; he did not even look at the lawyer; but his eyes were fixed on the old clergyman, with a profound expression of sorrow.

''There is an answer to that,'' he said. ''But I would much rather give it to anybody except Mr. Whiteways.''

And, strangely enough perhaps, the moment Mr. Whiteways heard this refusal he rose also and held out his hand to Gahagan.

''I believe you,'' he said. ''It's just that last sentence that has made me believe you.''

The scornful solicitor, being thus deserted by his own client, stuffed his papers back into his little black bag; and the irregular conference broke up.

Gahagan did tell the truth about the last question afterwards, to the person to whom he told everything, to Joan Varney, to whom he was engaged. And, queer as it sounded, she seemed to understand.

''If you like to put it so,'' he said, ''I didn't run away from the police; I ran away from the girl. And I know it sounds mad; but I really felt at the moment I was doing my best for her, in a beastly situation and among a lot of beastly alternatives. I knew by next morning that the vicar was saying he had seen me commit murder. Suppose I contradicted it—well, to begin with, she would have to know that her old friend, the friend of her pets, was a horrible lunatic who had offered her a sort of disgusting insult at the best.

''But it wasn't only that. I had behaved as badly as anybody; I was in a shamefully false position; and, if I remained, there was nothing before us but crawling through all that mire of miserable explanation and hopeless remorse, in which it is hard to say whether the man or the woman has the worst of it. And then a queer thought came to me—a secret, almost subconscious thought; but I couldn't get rid of the notion. Suppose she went on thinking, and remembered afterwards, in calmer times, that one man had killed another for her. She would be horrified; but she would not be humiliated. A mad whisper kept on repeating to me that in the long run she would be—a little proud."

"I think you're right about her," said Joan, in her straight way. "But, all the same, you ought to have told her the truth."

"Joan," he said, "I simply hadn't the courage."

"I know," she said. "I also know all about your having the D.S.O.; and I've seen you, myself, jump a chasm it made me sick to look at. But that's what's the matter with all you fine, fighting gentlemen." Her head lifted very slightly. "You haven't the courage."

A TALL STORY

THEY HAD BEEN DISCUSSING the new troubles in Germany: the three old friends, Sir Hubert Wotton, the famous official; Mr. Pond, the obscure official; and Captain Gahagan, who never did a stroke of work in the way of putting pen to paper, but liked making up the most fantastic stories on the spur of the moment. On this occasion, however, the group was increased to four; for Gahagan's wife was present, a candid-looking young woman with light-brown hair and dark-brown eyes. They had only just recently been married; and the presence of Joan Gahagan still stimulated the Captain to rather excessive flights of showing-off.

Captain Gahagan looked like a Regency buck; Mr. Pond looked like a round-eyed fish, with the beard and brow of Socrates; Sir Hubert Wotton looked like Sir Hubert Wotton—it summed up a very sound and virile quality in him, for which his friends had a great respect.

"It's an infernal shame," Wotton was saying, "the way these fellows have treated the Jews: perfectly decent and harmless Jews, who were no more Communists than I am; little men who'd worked their way up by merit and industry, all kicked out of their posts without a penny of compensation. Surely you agree with that, Gahagan?"

"Of course I do," replied Gahagan. "I never kicked a Jew. I can distinctly remember three and a half occasions on which I definitely refrained from doing so. As for all those hundreds and thousands of poor little fiddlers and actors and chess-players, I think it was a damned shame that they should be kicked out or kicked at all. But I fancy they must be kicking themselves, for having been so faithful to Germany and even, everywhere else, pretty generally pro-German."

"Even that can be exaggerated," said Mr. Pond. "Do you remember the case of Carl Schiller, that happened during the War? It was all kept rather quiet, as I have reason to know; for the thing happened, in some sense, in my department. I have generally found spy stories the dullest of all forms of detective fiction; in my own modest researches into the light literature of murder, I invariably avoid them. But this story really did have an unexpected and rather astonishing ending. Of course, you know that in wartime the official dealing with these things is very much exposed to amateurs, as the Duke of Wellington was exposed to authors. We persecuted the spies; and the spy-maniacs persecuted us. They were always coming to us to say they had seen certain persons who looked like spies. We vainly assured them that spies do not look like spies. As a matter of fact, the enemy was pretty ingenious in keeping the really suspicious character just out of sight; sometimes by his being ordinary; sometimes actually by his being extraordinary; one would be too small to be noticed, another too tall to be seen; one was apparently paralysed in a hospital and got out of the window at night——"

Joan looked across at him with a troubled expression in her honest brown eyes.

"Please, Mr. Pond, do tell us what you mean by a man being too tall to be seen."

Gahagan's spirits, already high, soared into laughter and light improvisation.

"These things do happen, my dear girl," he said. "I can throw out a thousand instances that would meet the case. Take, for example, the case of my unfortunate friends the Balham-Browns who lived at Muswell Hill. Mr. Balham-Brown had just come home from the office (of the Imperial and International Lead-Piping Company) and was exercising the lawn-mower in the usual manner, when he noticed in the grass a growth not green but reddish-brown and resembling animal hair; nay, even human hair. My friend Mr. Pond, whose private collection of Giant Whiskers is unrivalled (except, of course, by the unique collection of Sir Samuel Snodd), was able to identify it with the long hair of the Anakin; and judged by its vigour, the son of Anak was buried but still alive. With the spitefulness of the scientific world, Professor Pooter countered with the theory that Jupiter buried the Titans, one under Etna, another under Ossa, and a third under

Muswell Hill. Anyhow, the villa of my ill-fated friends the Balham-Browns was ruined, and the whole suburb overturned as by an earthquake, in order to excavate the monster. When his head alone emerged, it was like a colossal sphinx; and Mrs. Balham-Brown complained to the authorities that the face frightened her, because it was too large. Mr. Pond, who happened to be passing at the moment, immediately produced a paradox (of which he always carries a small supply) and said that, on the contrary, they would soon find that the face was too small. To cut a long story short——"

"Or a tall story shorter," said Joan in a trenchant manner.

"When the Titan was extricated, he was so tall that by the common converging laws of perspective, his head in the remote sky was a mere dot. It was impossible to discern or recall one feature of that old familiar face. He strode away; and fortunately decided to walk across the Atlantic, where even he was apparently submerged. It is believed that the unfortunate creature was going to give lectures in America; driven by that mysterious instinct which leads any person who is notorious for any reason to adopt that course."

"Well, have you done?" demanded Joan. "We know all about you and your yarns; and they don't mean anything. But when Mr. Pond says that somebody was too tall to be seen, he does mean something. And what can he possibly mean?"

"Well," said Mr. Pond, coughing slightly, "it was really a part of the story to which I was alluding just now. I did not notice anything odd about the expression when I used it; but I recognize, on second thought, that it is, perhaps, a phrase requiring explanation." And he proceeded, in his slightly pedantic way, to narrate the story which is now retold here.

It all happened in a fashionable watering-place, which was also a famous seaport, and, therefore, naturally a place of concentration for all the vigilance against spies, whether official or amateur. Sir Hubert Wotton was in general charge of the district, but Mr. Pond was in more practical though private occupation of the town, watching events from a narrow house in a back street, an upper room of which had been unobtrusively turned into an office; and he had two assistants under him; a sturdy and very silent young man named Butt, bull-necked and broad-shouldered, but quite short; and a much taller and more talkative and elegant government-office clerk named Travers, but referred to by nearly everybody as Arthur. The stalwart Butt commonly occupied a desk on the ground floor, watching the door and anyone who entered it; while Arthur Travers worked in the office upstairs, where there were some very valuable State papers, including the only plan of the mines in the harbour.

Mr. Pond himself always spent several hours in the office, but he had more occasion than the others to pay visits in the town, and had a general grasp of the neighbourhood. It was a very shabby neighbourhood; indeed, it consisted of a few genteel, old-fashioned houses, now mostly shuttered and empty, standing on the very edge of a sort of slum of small houses, at that time riddled with what is called Unrest in a degree very dangerous, especially in time of war. Immediately outside his door, he found but few things that could be called features in that featureless street; but there was an old curiosity shop opposite, with a display of ancient Asiatic weapons; and there was Mrs. Hartog-Haggard next door, more alarming than all the weapons of the world.

Mrs. Hartog-Haggard was one of those persons, to be found here and there, who look like the conventional caricature of the spinster, though they are in fact excellent mothers of families. Rather in the same way, she looked very like the sort of lady who is horribly in earnest at Pacifist meetings; yet, as a matter of fact, she was passionately patriotic, not to say militaristic. And, indeed, it is often true that those two extremes lend themselves to the same sort of fluent fanaticism. Poor Mr. Pond had reason to remember the woeful day when he first saw her angular and agitated figure darkening his doorway as she entered out of the street, peering suspiciously through her curious square spectacles. There was apparently some slight delay about her entrance; some repairs were being done to the porch and some loose board or pole was not removed sufficiently promptly from her path: was, in fact, as she declared, removed reluctantly and in a grumbling spirit by the workmen employed on the job; and by the time she had reached the responsible official, a theory had fully formed and hardened in her mind.

"That man is a *Socialist*, Mr. Pond," she declared in the ear of that unfortunate functionary. "I heard him with my own ears mutter something about what his Trade Union would say. What is he doing so near to your office?"

"We must distinguish," said Mr. Pond. "A Trade Unionist, even a militant Trade Unionist, is not necessarily a Socialist; a Socialist is not necessarily a Pacifist, still less a Pro-German. In my opinion, the chief S.D.F. men are the most extreme Marxians in England; and they are all out for the Allies. One of the Dock Strike leaders is in a mood to make recruiting speeches all over the Empire."

"I'm sure he's not English; he doesn't look a bit English," said the lady, still thinking of her wicked proletarian without.

"Thank you, Mrs. Hartog-Haggard," said Pond, patiently. "I will certainly make a note of your warning and see that inquiries are made about it."

And so he did, with the laborious precision of one who could not leave any loophole unguarded. Certainly the man did not look very English; though perhaps rather Scandinavian than German. His name was Peterson: it was possible that it was really Petersen. But that was not all. Mr. Pond had learned the last lesson of the wise man: that the fool is sometimes right.

He soon forgot the incident in the details of his work; and next day it was with a start that he looked up from his desk, or rather from Mr. Butt's desk which he was using at the moment, and saw once again the patriotic lady hovering like an avenging shadow in the doorway. This time she glided swiftly in, unchecked by any Socialist barricade, and warned him that she had news of the most terrible kind. She seemed to have forgotten all about her last suspicions; and, in truth, her new ones were naturally more important to her. This time she had warmed the viper on her own hearth. She had suddenly become conscious of the existence of her own German governess, whom she had never especially noticed before. Pond himself had noticed the alien in question with rather more attention; he had seen her, a dumpy lady with pale hair, returning with Mrs. Hartog-Haggard's three little girls and one little boy from the pantomime of Puss-in-Boots that was being performed on the pier. He had even heard her instructing her charges, and saying something educational about a folk-tale; and had smiled faintly at that touch of Teutonic pedantry that talks about a folk-tale when we would talk about a fairy-tale. But he knew a good deal about the lady; and saw no reason to move in the matter.

"She shuts herself up for hours in her room and won't come out," Mrs. Hartog-Haggard was already breathing hoarsely in his ear. "Do you think she is signalling, or does she climb down the fire-escape? What do you think it means, Mr. Pond?"

"Hysterics," said Mr. Pond. "What, do you think the poor lady cannot be hysterical, because she does not scream the house down? But any doctor will tell you that hysteria is mostly secretive and silent. And there really is a vein of hysteria in a great many of the Germans; it is at the very opposite extreme to the external excitability of the Latins. No, madam, I do not think she is climbing down the fire-escape. I think she is saying that her pupils do not love her, and thinking about *weltschmerz* and suicide. And really, poor woman, she is in a very hard position."

"She won't come to family prayers," continued the patriotic matron, not to be turned from her course, "because we pray for a British victory."

"You had better pray," said Mr. Pond, "for all the unhappy Englishwomen stranded in Germany by poverty or duty or dependence. If she loves her native land, it only shows she is a human being. If she expresses it by ostentatious absences or sulks or banging doors, that may show she is too much of a German. It also shows she is not much of a German spy."

Here again, however, Mr. Pond was careful not to ignore or entirely despise the warning; he kept an eye on the German governess, and even engaged that learned lady in talk upon some trivial pretext—if anything she touched could remain trivial.

"Your study of our national drama," he said gravely, "must sometimes recall to you the greatest and noblest work that ever came out of Germany."

"You refer to Goethe's *Faust,* I presume," she replied.

"I refer to Grimm's Fairy-Tales," said Mr. Pond. "I fear I have forgotten for the moment whether the story we call *Puss-in-Boots* exists in Grimm's collection in the same form; but I am pretty certain there is some variant of it. It always seems to me about the best story in the world."

The German governess obliged him with a short lecture on the parallelism of folk-lore; and Pond could not help feeling faintly amused at the idea of this ethnological and scientific treatment of a folk-tale which had just been presented on the pier by Miss Patsy Pickles, in tights and various other embellishments, supported by that world-famed comedian who called himself Alberto Tizzi and was born in the Blackfriars Road.

When he returned to his office at twilight, and, turning, beheld the figure of Mrs. Hartog-Haggard again hovering without, Mr. Pond began to think he was in a nightmare. He wondered wildly whether she had drawn some dark conclusions from his own meeting with the Teutonic teacher of youth. Perhaps he, Mr. Pond, was a German spy, too. But he ought to have known his neighbour better; for when Mrs. Hartog-Haggard spoke she had once again forgotten, for the moment, her last cause of complaint. But she was more excited than ever; she ducked under the frame of scaffolding and darted into the room, crying out as she came:

"Mr. Pond, do you know what is right opposite your own house?"

"Well, I think so," said Mr. Pond, doubtfully, "more or less."

"I never read the name over the shop before!" cried the lady. "You know it is all dark and dirty and obliterated—that curiosity shop, I mean; with all the spears and daggers. Think of the impudence of the man! He's actually written up his name there: 'C. Schiller.' "

"He's written up C. Schiller; I'm not so sure he's written up his name," said Mr. Pond.

"Do you mean," she cried, "that you actually know he goes by two names? Why, that makes it worse than ever!"

"Well," said Mr. Pond, rising suddenly, and with a curtness that cut all his own courtesy, "I'll see what I can do about it."

And for the third time did Mr. Pond take some steps to verify the Hartog-Haggard revelations. He took the ten or twelve steps necessary to take him across the road and into the shop of C. Schiller, amid all the shining sabres and yataghans. It was a very peaceable-looking person who waited behind all this array of arms; not to say a rather smooth and sleek one; and Pond, leaning across the counter, addressed him in a low and confidential voice.

"Why the dickens do you people do it? It will be more than half your own fault if there's a row of some kind and a Jingo mob comes here and breaks your windows for your absurd German name. I know very well this is no quarrel of yours. I am well aware," Mr. Pond continued with an earnest gaze, "that you never invaded Belgium. I am fully conscious that your national tastes do not lie in that direction. I know you had nothing to do with burning the Louvain Library or sinking the *Lusitania*. Then why the devil can't you say so? Why can't you call yourself Levy, like your fathers before you—your fathers who go back to the most ancient priesthood of the world? And you'll get into trouble with the Germans, too, some day, if you go about calling yourself Schiller. You might as well go and live in Stratford-on-Avon and call yourself Shakespeare."

"There'th a lot of prejudith againth my rathe," said the warden of the armoury.

"There'll be a lot more, unless you take my advice," said Mr. Pond with unusual brevity; and left the shop to return to the office.

The square figure of Mr. Butt, who was sitting at the desk looking towards the doorway, rose at his entrance; but Pond waved him to his seat again and, lighting a cigarette, began to moon about the room in a rather moody fashion. He did not believe that there was anything very much in any of the three avenues of suspicion that had been opened to him; though he owned that there were indirect possibilities about the last. Mr. Levy was certainly not a German; and it was very improbable that he was a real enthusiast for Germany; but it was not altogether impossible to suppose, in the tangle and distraction of all the modern international muddle, that he might be some sort of tool, conscious or unconscious, of a real German conspiracy. So long as that was possible, he must be watched. Mr. Pond was very glad that Mr. Levy lived in the shop exactly opposite.

Indeed, he found himself gazing across the street in the gathering dusk with feelings which he found it hard to analyse. He could still see the shop, with its pattern of queer, archaic weapons, through the frame of the last few poles left in the low scaffolding round the porch; for the workmen's business had been entirely limited to the porch itself and the props were mostly cleared away, the work being practically over; but there was just enough suggestion of a cluster or network of lines to confuse the prospect at that very confusing turn of the twilight. Once he fancied he saw something flicker behind them, as if a shadow had shifted; and there arose within him the terror of Mrs. Hartog-Haggard, which is the terror of boredom and a sort of paralysed impatience, one of the worst of the woes of life.

Then he saw that the shifting shadow must have been produced by the fact that the lights had been turned up in the shop opposite; and he saw again, and now much more clearly, the queer outline of all those alien Asiatic weapons, the crooked darts and monstrous missiles, the swords with a horrid resemblance to hooks or the blades that bent back and forth like snakes of iron. . . . He became dreamily conscious of the chasm between Christendom and that great other half of human civilization; so dreamily that he hardly knew which was a torture implement and which was a tool. Whether the thought was mingled with his own belief that he was fighting a barbarism at heart as hostile, or whether he had caught a whiff of the strange smell of the East from that apparently harmless human accident who kept the shop, he could hardly be certain himself; but he felt the peculiar oppression of his work as he had never felt it before.

Then he shook himself awake, telling himself sharply that his business was working and not worrying about the atmosphere of the work; and that he should be ashamed to idle when his two subordinates were still busy, Butt behind him, and Travers in the office above. He was all the more surprised, when he turned sharply around, to find that Butt was not working at all; but, like himself, was staring, not to say glaring, as in a congested mystification, into the twilight. Butt was commonly the most calm and prosaic of subordinates; but the look on his face was quite enough to prove that something was really the matter.

"Is anything bothering you?" asked Pond, in a gentle voice which people found very encouraging.

"Yes, sir," said Mr. Butt. "I'm bothering about whether I'm going to be a beast or not. It's a beastly caddish thing to say a word, or hint a word, against your comrades or anybody connected with them. But after all—well, sir, there is the country, isn't there?"

"There is certainly the country," said Mr. Pond, very seriously.

"Well," Butt blurted out at last, "I'm not a bit comfortable about Arthur."

Then, after a sort of gasp, he tried again: "At least, it isn't so much Arthur as Arthur's . . . what Arthur's doing. It makes it all the nastier to have put it like that. But you know he got engaged last week. Have you met his fiancée, sir?"

"I have not yet had the honour," replied Pond, in his punctilious way.

"Well, sir, Arthur brought her in here to-day while you were out; he'd just taken her to the pantomime of Puss-in-Boots on the pier, and they were laughing like anything. Of course, that's quite all right; it was his off time; but it seemed to me it wasn't quite all right that she walked straight upstairs without any invitation, even from him, to the private office where we don't allow visitors to go. Of course, that's about the only possible case where I could hardly prevent it. In the ordinary way, we're perfectly safe; I mean the documents are perfectly safe. There's only one door, and you or I are always sitting bang in front of it; and there's only one staircase, and nobody uses it but we three. Of course, she might have done it in all innocence; that's what made it seem quite too ghastly to snub her. And yet. . . . Well, she's a very nice-looking girl, and no doubt a very nice girl; but somehow that's just the one word that wouldn't jump to my mind about her—innocence."

"Why, what sort of a girl is she?" asked Pond.

"Well," said Mr. Butt, gloomily seeking words, "we all know that making-up and even dyeing your hair doesn't mean what it once did; lots of women do it who are perfectly decent; but not those who are—well, utterly inexperienced. It seemed to me that, while she might be perfectly honest, she *would* know very decidedly whether a thing is done or not."

"If she is engaged to him," said Pond, with a rather unusual severity, "she must know that he is here on highly confidential work, and she must be as anxious to protect his honour as we are. I'm afraid that I shall have to ask you for some sort of description."

"Well," said Butt, "she's very tall and elegant, or . . . no, elegant is exactly the word. She has beautiful golden hair—very beautiful golden hair—and very beautiful long dark eyes that make it look rather like a gilded wig. She has high cheekbones, not in the way that Scotch girls have, but somehow as if it were part of the shape of the skull; and though she's not at all long in the tooth, in any sense, her teeth are just a little to the fore."

"Did he meet her in Besançon, near Belfort?"

"Pretty rum you should say that," said Butt, miserably; "because he did."

Mr. Pond received the news in silence.

"I hope, sir, you won't assume anything against Arthur," said Butt, huskily. "I'm sure I'd do anything to clear him of any——"

As he spoke, the ceiling above them shook with a thud like thunder; then there was a sound of scampering feet; and then utter stillness. No one acquainted with Mr. Pond's usual process of ambulation could have believed that he flew up the staircase as he did just then.

They flung open the door, and they saw all that was to be seen. All that was to be seen was Arthur Travers stretched out face downwards on the ground, and between his shoulder-blades stood out the very long hilt of a very strange-looking sword. Butt impetuously laid hold of it, and was startled to find that it was sunk so deep in the corpse and the carpeted floor that he could not have plucked it out without the most violent muscular effort. Pond had already touched the wrist and felt the rigidity of the muscles and he waved his subordinate away.

"I am sorry to say that our friend is certainly dead," he said steadily. "In that case, you had better not touch things till they can be properly examined." Then, looking at Butt very solemnly, he added:

"You said you would do anything to clear him. One thing is certain: that he is quite cleared."

Pond then walked in silence to the desk, which contained the secret drawer and the secret plan of the harbour. He only compressed his lips when he saw that the drawer was empty.

Pond walked to the telephone and issued orders to about six different people. He did about twenty things, but he did not speak again for about three-quarters of an hour. It was only about the same time that the stunned and bewildered Butt stumbled into speech.

"I simply can't make head or tail of anything. That woman had gone; and, besides, no woman could have nailed him to the floor like that."

"And with such an extraordinary nail," said Pond, and was silent once more.

And indeed the riddle revolved more and more on the one thing that thief and murderer had left behind him: the enormous misshapen weapon. It was not difficult to guess why he had left it behind; it was so difficult to tug out of the floor that he probably had no time to try effectually, hearing Pond clattering up the stairs; he thought it wiser to escape somehow, presumably through the window. But about the nature of the thing itself it was hard to say anything, for it seemed quite abnormal. It was as long as a claymore; yet it was not upon the pattern of any known sword. It had no guard or pommel of any kind. The hilt was as long as the blade; the blade was twice as broad as the hilt; at least, at its base, whence it tapered to a point in a sort of right-angled triangle, only the outer edge or hypotenuse being sharpened. Pond gazed musingly at this uncouth weapon, which was made very rudely of iron and wood painted with garish colours; and his thoughts crept slowly back to that shop across the road that was hung with strange and savage weapons. Yet this seemed to be in a somewhat cruder and gaudier style. Mr. Schiller-Levy naturally denied all knowledge of it, which he would presumably have done in any case; but what was much more cogent, all the real authorities on such barbaric or Oriental arms said that they had never seen such a thing before.

Touching many other things, the darkness began to thin away to a somewhat dreary dawn. It was ascertained that poor Arthur's equivocal fiancée had indeed fled; very possibly in company with the missing plan. She was known by this time to be a woman quite capable of stealing a document or even stabbing a man. But it was doubtful whether any woman was capable of stabbing a man, with that huge and heavy and clumsy instrument, so as to fix him to the floor; and quite impossible to imagine why she should select it for the purpose.

"It would all be as clear as death," said Mr. Butt, bitterly, "except for that lumbering, long-hilted short-sword, or whatever it is. It never was in Levy's shop. It never was in Asia or Africa or any of the tribes the learned jossers tell us about. It's the real remaining mystery of the whole thing."

Mr. Pond seemed to be waking up slowly from a trance of hours or days.

"Oh, *that*," he said, "that's the only thing about it I'm really beginning to understand."

It has been hinted, with every delicacy, we may hope, that the attitude of Mr. Pond towards the visits of Mrs. Hartog-Haggard was, perhaps, rather passive than receptive; that he did not look forward to them as pants the hart for cooling streams; and that for him they rather resembled getting into hot water. It is all the more worthy of record that, on the last occasion of her bringing him a new tale of woe, he actually leapt to his feet with an air of excitement and even of triumph. He had been right in his premonitions about the wisdom of folly; and the triumph was truly the triumph of the fool. Mrs. Hartog-Haggard gave him the clue after all.

She darted in under the scaffolding by the doorway, the same dark and almost antic figure. Full of the Cause, she was utterly oblivious of such trifles as the murder of his friend. She had now reverted to her original disapproval of her own governess. She had altered nothing, except all her reasons for disapproving of her governess. On the former occasion she had appeared to claim the fairy-tale used for pantomimes as exclusively English and part of the healthy innocence of the stately homes of England. Now she was denouncing the German woman for taking the children to the pantomime at all; regarding it as a ruse for filling them with the gruesome tales of Grimm and the terrors of the barbaric forest.

"They're *sent* to do that," she repeated in the fierce, confidential voice she used in such cases. "They're sent here to undermine all our children's nerves and minds. Could any other nation be such fiends, Mr. Pond? She's been poisoning their poor little minds with horrors about magicians and magic cats; and now the worst has happened, as I knew it would. Well—*you* haven't done anything to stop it; and my life is simply ruined. My three girls are all twittering with terror; and my boy is mad."

The symptoms of Mr. Pond were still mainly those of fatigue; and she rapped out a repetition.

"He is *mad*, I tell you, Mr. Pond; he is actually *seeing* things out of those horrible German fairy-tales; says he saw a giant with a great knife walking through the town by moonlight . . . a *giant*, Mr. Pond."

Mr. Pond staggered to his feet and for once really goggled and gulped like a fish. Mrs. Hartog-Haggard watched him with wild eyes, intermittently exclaiming: "Have you no word of consolation for a mother?"

Mr. Pond abruptly controlled himself and managed to recapture, at least, a hazy courtesy.

"Yes, madam," he said. "I have the best possible consolation for a mother. Your son is not mad."

He looked more judicial, and even severe, when he next sat in consultation with Mr. Butt, Sir Hubert Wotton, and Inspector Grote, the leading detective of the district.

"What it comes to is this," said Mr. Pond, very sternly: "that you do not really know the story of Puss-in-Boots. And they talk about this as an epoch of Education."

"Oh, I know it's about a clever cat and all the rest of it," said Butt, vaguely. "A cat that helps its master to get things——"

The Inspector smote his knee with a smack that rang through the office.

"A cat burglar!" he cried. "So that's what you mean. I fancied at first there was something wrong about that bit of scaffolding round the door; but I soon saw it was far too low and small for anybody to climb up to the window by it. But, of course, if we're talking about a really clever cat burglar, there's always some chance that——"

"Pardon me," said Mr. Pond, "does a cat burglar, or for that matter any burglar, any more than any cat, load himself with a gigantic knife rather bigger than a garden spade? Nobody carries a gigantic knife except a giant. This crime was committed by a giant."

They all stared at him; but he resumed with the same air of frigid rebuke:

"What I remark upon, what I regret and regard as symptomatic of serious intellectual decay, is that you apparently do not know that the story of Puss-in-Boots includes a giant. He is also a magician; but he is always depicted, in pictures and pantomimes, as an ogre with a large knife. Signor Alberto Tizzi, that somewhat dubious foreign artist, enacts the part on the pier by the usual expedient of walking on very high stilts, covered by very long trousers. But he sometimes walks about on the stilts and dispenses with the trousers; taking a walk through the almost entirely deserted streets at night. Just round here, especially, the chances are against his being even seen; all the big houses are shut up, except ours and Mrs. Hartog-Haggard's, which only looks on the street through a landing window; through which her little boy (probably in his nightgown) peered and beheld a real ogre, with a great gory knife, and, perhaps, a great grinning mask, walking majestically under the moon—rather a fine sight to put among the memories of childhood. For the rest, all the poor houses are low houses of one story; and the people would see nothing but his legs, or rather his stilts, even if they did look out; and they probably didn't. The really native poor, in these seaport towns, have country habits; and generally go to bed early. But it wouldn't really have been fatal to his plans even if he had been seen. He was a recognized public entertainer, dressed in his recognized part; and there is nothing illegal in walking about on stilts. The really clever part of it was the trick by which he could leave the stilts standing, and climb out of them on to any ledge or roof or other upper level. So he left them standing outside our doorway, among the poles of the little scaffolding, while he climbed in at the upper window and killed poor Travers."

"If you are sure of this," cried Sir Hubert Wotton, starting to his feet hastily, "you ought to act on it at once!"

"I did act on it at once," replied Pond, with a slight sigh. "This morning two or three clowns with white faces were going about on stilts on the beach, distributing leaflets of the pantomime. One of them was arrested and found to be Signor Tizzi. He was also found, I am glad to say, to be still in possession of the plans." But he sighed again.

"For after all," as Mr. Pond observed, in telling the tale long after, "though we did manage to save the secret plans, the incident was much more of a tragedy than a triumph. And what I most intensely disliked about the tragedy was the irony—what I believe is called the tragic irony, or, alternatively, the Greek irony. We felt perfectly certain we were guarding the only entrance to the office, because we sat staring at the street between two little clusters of sticks, which we knew were a temporary part of the furniture. We didn't count the sticks; we didn't know when there happened to be two more wooden poles standing up among the other wooden poles. We certainly had no notion of what was on top of those two poles; nor would our fancy have easily entertained the idea that it was a pantomime giant. We ought to have seen him—only," said Mr. Pond, ending, as he had begun, with an apologetic little laugh, "he was too tall to be seen."

A CATALOG OF SELECTED

DOVER BOOKS

IN ALL FIELDS OF INTEREST

A CATALOG OF SELECTED DOVER
BOOKS IN ALL FIELDS OF INTEREST

DRAWINGS OF REMBRANDT, edited by Seymour Slive. Updated Lippmann, Hofstede de Groot edition, with definitive scholarly apparatus. All portraits, biblical sketches, landscapes, nudes. Oriental figures, classical studies, together with selection of work by followers. 550 illustrations. Total of 630pp. 9⅛ × 12¼.
21485-0, 21486-9 Pa., Two-vol. set $25.00

GHOST AND HORROR STORIES OF AMBROSE BIERCE, Ambrose Bierce. 24 tales vividly imagined, strangely prophetic, and decades ahead of their time in technical skill: "The Damned Thing," "An Inhabitant of Carcosa," "The Eyes of the Panther," "Moxon's Master," and 20 more. 199pp. 5⅜ × 8½. 20767-6 Pa. $3.95

ETHICAL WRITINGS OF MAIMONIDES, Maimonides. Most significant ethical works of great medieval sage, newly translated for utmost precision, readability. Laws Concerning Character Traits, Eight Chapters, more. 192pp. 5⅜ × 8½.
24522-5 Pa. $4.50

THE EXPLORATION OF THE COLORADO RIVER AND ITS CANYONS, J. W. Powell. Full text of Powell's 1,000-mile expedition down the fabled Colorado in 1869. Superb account of terrain, geology, vegetation, Indians, famine, mutiny, treacherous rapids, mighty canyons, during exploration of last unknown part of continental U.S. 400pp. 5⅜ × 8½. 20094-9 Pa. $6.95

HISTORY OF PHILOSOPHY, Julián Marías. Clearest one-volume history on the market. Every major philosopher and dozens of others, to Existentialism and later. 505pp. 5⅜ × 8½. 21739-6 Pa. $8.50

ALL ABOUT LIGHTNING, Martin A. Uman. Highly readable non-technical survey of nature and causes of lightning, thunderstorms, ball lightning, St. Elmo's Fire, much more. Illustrated. 192pp. 5⅜ × 8½. 25237-X Pa. $5.95

SAILING ALONE AROUND THE WORLD, Captain Joshua Slocum. First man to sail around the world, alone, in small boat. One of great feats of seamanship told in delightful manner. 67 illustrations. 294pp. 5⅜ × 8½. 20326-3 Pa. $4.95

LETTERS AND NOTES ON THE MANNERS, CUSTOMS AND CONDITIONS OF THE NORTH AMERICAN INDIANS, George Catlin. Classic account of life among Plains Indians: ceremonies, hunt, warfare, etc. 312 plates. 572pp. of text. 6⅛ × 9¼. 22118-0, 22119-9 Pa. Two-vol. set $15.90

ALASKA: The Harriman Expedition, 1899, John Burroughs, John Muir, et al. Informative, engrossing accounts of two-month, 9,000-mile expedition. Native peoples, wildlife, forests, geography, salmon industry, glaciers, more. Profusely illustrated. 240 black-and-white line drawings. 124 black-and-white photographs. 3 maps. Index. 576pp. 5⅜ × 8½. 25109-8 Pa. $11.95

THE BOOK OF BEASTS: Being a Translation from a Latin Bestiary of the Twelfth Century, T. H. White. Wonderful catalog real and fanciful beasts: manticore, griffin, phoenix, amphivius, jaculus, many more. White's witty erudite commentary on scientific, historical aspects. Fascinating glimpse of medieval mind. Illustrated. 296pp. 5⅜ × 8¼. (Available in U.S. only) 24609-4 Pa. $5.95

FRANK LLOYD WRIGHT: ARCHITECTURE AND NATURE With 160 Illustrations, Donald Hoffmann. Profusely illustrated study of influence of nature—especially prairie—on Wright's designs for Fallingwater, Robie House, Guggenheim Museum, other masterpieces. 96pp. 9¼ × 10¾. 25098-9 Pa. $7.95

FRANK LLOYD WRIGHT'S FALLINGWATER, Donald Hoffmann. Wright's famous waterfall house: planning and construction of organic idea. History of site, owners, Wright's personal involvement. Photographs of various stages of building. Preface by Edgar Kaufmann, Jr. 100 illustrations. 112pp. 9¼ × 10.
23671-4 Pa. $7.95

YEARS WITH FRANK LLOYD WRIGHT: Apprentice to Genius, Edgar Tafel. Insightful memoir by a former apprentice presents a revealing portrait of Wright the man, the inspired teacher, the greatest American architect. 372 black-and-white illustrations. Preface. Index. vi + 228pp. 8¼ × 11. 24801-1 Pa. $9.95

THE STORY OF KING ARTHUR AND HIS KNIGHTS, Howard Pyle. Enchanting version of King Arthur fable has delighted generations with imaginative narratives of exciting adventures and unforgettable illustrations by the author. 41 illustrations. xviii + 313pp. 6⅛ × 9¼. 21445-1 Pa. $5.95

THE GODS OF THE EGYPTIANS, E. A. Wallis Budge. Thorough coverage of numerous gods of ancient Egypt by foremost Egyptologist. Information on evolution of cults, rites and gods; the cult of Osiris; the Book of the Dead and its rites; the sacred animals and birds; Heaven and Hell; and more. 956pp. 6⅛ × 9¼.
22055-9, 22056-7 Pa., Two-vol. set $21.90

A THEOLOGICO-POLITICAL TREATISE, Benedict Spinoza. Also contains unfinished *Political Treatise*. Great classic on religious liberty, theory of government on common consent. R. Elwes translation. Total of 421pp. 5⅜ × 8½.
20249-6 Pa. $6.95

INCIDENTS OF TRAVEL IN CENTRAL AMERICA, CHIAPAS, AND YUCATAN, John L. Stephens. Almost single-handed discovery of Maya culture; exploration of ruined cities, monuments, temples; customs of Indians. 115 drawings. 892pp. 5⅜ × 8½. 22404-X, 22405-8 Pa., Two-vol. set $15.90

LOS CAPRICHOS, Francisco Goya. 80 plates of wild, grotesque monsters and caricatures. Prado manuscript included. 183pp. 6⅜ × 9⅜. 22384-1 Pa. $4.95

AUTOBIOGRAPHY: The Story of My Experiments with Truth, Mohandas K. Gandhi. Not hagiography, but Gandhi in his own words. Boyhood, legal studies, purification, the growth of the Satyagraha (nonviolent protest) movement. Critical, inspiring work of the man who freed India. 480pp. 5⅜ × 8½. (Available in U.S. only)
24593-4 Pa. $6.95

ILLUSTRATED DICTIONARY OF HISTORIC ARCHITECTURE, edited by Cyril M. Harris. Extraordinary compendium of clear, concise definitions for over 5,000 important architectural terms complemented by over 2,000 line drawings. Covers full spectrum of architecture from ancient ruins to 20th-century Modernism. Preface. 592pp. 7½ × 9⅝. 24444-X Pa. $14.95

THE NIGHT BEFORE CHRISTMAS, Clement Moore. Full text, and woodcuts from original 1848 book. Also critical, historical material. 19 illustrations. 40pp. 4⅝ × 6. 22797-9 Pa. $2.50

THE LESSON OF JAPANESE ARCHITECTURE: 165 Photographs, Jiro Harada. Memorable gallery of 165 photographs taken in the 1930's of exquisite Japanese homes of the well-to-do and historic buildings. 13 line diagrams. 192pp. 8⅜ × 11¼. 24778-3 Pa. $8.95

THE AUTOBIOGRAPHY OF CHARLES DARWIN AND SELECTED LETTERS, edited by Francis Darwin. The fascinating life of eccentric genius composed of an intimate memoir by Darwin (intended for his children); commentary by his son, Francis; hundreds of fragments from notebooks, journals, papers; and letters to and from Lyell, Hooker, Huxley, Wallace and Henslow. xi + 365pp. 5⅜ × 8. 20479-0 Pa. $5.95

WONDERS OF THE SKY: Observing Rainbows, Comets, Eclipses, the Stars and Other Phenomena, Fred Schaaf. Charming, easy-to-read poetic guide to all manner of celestial events visible to the naked eye. Mock suns, glories, Belt of Venus, more. Illustrated. 299pp. 5¼ × 8¼. 24402-4 Pa. $7.95

BURNHAM'S CELESTIAL HANDBOOK, Robert Burnham, Jr. Thorough guide to the stars beyond our solar system. Exhaustive treatment. Alphabetical by constellation: Andromeda to Cetus in Vol. 1; Chamaeleon to Orion in Vol. 2; and Pavo to Vulpecula in Vol. 3. Hundreds of illustrations. Index in Vol. 3. 2,000pp. 6⅛ × 9¼. 23567-X, 23568-8, 23673-0 Pa., Three-vol. set $37.85

STAR NAMES: Their Lore and Meaning, Richard Hinckley Allen. Fascinating history of names various cultures have given to constellations and literary and folkloristic uses that have been made of stars. Indexes to subjects. Arabic and Greek names. Biblical references. Bibliography. 563pp. 5⅜ × 8½. 21079-0 Pa. $7.95

THIRTY YEARS THAT SHOOK PHYSICS: The Story of Quantum Theory, George Gamow. Lucid, accessible introduction to influential theory of energy and matter. Careful explanations of Dirac's anti-particles, Bohr's model of the atom, much more. 12 plates. Numerous drawings. 240pp. 5⅜ × 8½. 24895-X Pa. $4.95

CHINESE DOMESTIC FURNITURE IN PHOTOGRAPHS AND MEASURED DRAWINGS, Gustav Ecke. A rare volume, now affordably priced for antique collectors, furniture buffs and art historians. Detailed review of styles ranging from early Shang to late Ming. Unabridged republication. 161 black-and-white drawings, photos. Total of 224pp. 8⅜ × 11¼. (Available in U.S. only) 25171-3 Pa. $12.95

VINCENT VAN GOGH: A Biography, Julius Meier-Graefe. Dynamic, penetrating study of artist's life, relationship with brother, Theo, painting techniques, travels, more. Readable, engrossing. 160pp. 5⅜ × 8½. (Available in U.S. only) 25253-1 Pa. $3.95

HOW TO WRITE, Gertrude Stein. Gertrude Stein claimed anyone could understand her unconventional writing—here are clues to help. Fascinating improvisations, language experiments, explanations illuminate Stein's craft and the art of writing. Total of 414pp. 4⅜ × 6⅜. 23144-5 Pa. $5.95

ADVENTURES AT SEA IN THE GREAT AGE OF SAIL: Five Firsthand Narratives, edited by Elliot Snow. Rare true accounts of exploration, whaling, shipwreck, fierce natives, trade, shipboard life, more. 33 illustrations. Introduction. 353pp. 5⅜ × 8½. 25177-2 Pa. $7.95

THE HERBAL OR GENERAL HISTORY OF PLANTS, John Gerard. Classic descriptions of about 2,850 plants—with over 2,700 illustrations—includes Latin and English names, physical descriptions, varieties, time and place of growth, more. 2,706 illustrations. xlv + 1,678pp. 8½ × 12¼. 23147-X Cloth. $75.00

DOROTHY AND THE WIZARD IN OZ, L. Frank Baum. Dorothy and the Wizard visit the center of the Earth, where people are vegetables, glass houses grow and Oz characters reappear. Classic sequel to *Wizard of Oz*. 256pp. 5⅜ × 8. 24714-7 Pa. $4.95

SONGS OF EXPERIENCE: Facsimile Reproduction with 26 Plates in Full Color, William Blake. This facsimile of Blake's original "Illuminated Book" reproduces 26 full-color plates from a rare 1826 edition. Includes "The Tyger," "London," "Holy Thursday," and other immortal poems. 26 color plates. Printed text of poems. 48pp. 5¼ × 7. 24636-1 Pa. $3.50

SONGS OF INNOCENCE, William Blake. The first and most popular of Blake's famous "Illuminated Books," in a facsimile edition reproducing all 31 brightly colored plates. Additional printed text of each poem. 64pp. 5¼ × 7. 22764-2 Pa. $3.50

PRECIOUS STONES, Max Bauer. Classic, thorough study of diamonds, rubies, emeralds, garnets, etc.: physical character, occurrence, properties, use, similar topics. 20 plates, 8 in color. 94 figures. 659pp. 6⅛ × 9¼. 21910-0, 21911-9 Pa., Two-vol. set $15.90

ENCYCLOPEDIA OF VICTORIAN NEEDLEWORK, S. F. A. Caulfeild and Blanche Saward. Full, precise descriptions of stitches, techniques for dozens of needlecrafts—most exhaustive reference of its kind. Over 800 figures. Total of 679pp. 8⅛ × 11. Two volumes. Vol. 1 22800-2 Pa. $11.95
Vol. 2 22801-0 Pa. $11.95

THE MARVELOUS LAND OF OZ, L. Frank Baum. Second Oz book, the Scarecrow and Tin Woodman are back with hero named Tip, Oz magic. 136 illustrations. 287pp. 5⅜ × 8½. 20692-0 Pa. $5.95

WILD FOWL DECOYS, Joel Barber. Basic book on the subject, by foremost authority and collector. Reveals history of decoy making and rigging, place in American culture, different kinds of decoys, how to make them, and how to use them. 140 plates. 156pp. 7⅞ × 10¾. 20011-6 Pa. $8.95

HISTORY OF LACE, Mrs. Bury Palliser. Definitive, profusely illustrated chronicle of lace from earliest times to late 19th century. Laces of Italy, Greece, England, France, Belgium, etc. Landmark of needlework scholarship. 266 illustrations. 672pp. 6⅛ × 9¼. 24742-2 Pa. $14.95

ILLUSTRATED GUIDE TO SHAKER FURNITURE, Robert Meader. All furniture and appurtenances, with much on unknown local styles. 235 photos. 146pp. 9 × 12. 22819-3 Pa. $7.95

WHALE SHIPS AND WHALING: A Pictorial Survey, George Francis Dow. Over 200 vintage engravings, drawings, photographs of barks, brigs, cutters, other vessels. Also harpoons, lances, whaling guns, many other artifacts. Comprehensive text by foremost authority. 207 black-and-white illustrations. 288pp. 6 × 9. 24808-9 Pa. $8.95

THE BERTRAMS, Anthony Trollope. Powerful portrayal of blind self-will and thwarted ambition includes one of Trollope's most heartrending love stories. 497pp. 5⅜ × 8½. 25119-5 Pa. $8.95

ADVENTURES WITH A HAND LENS, Richard Headstrom. Clearly written guide to observing and studying flowers and grasses, fish scales, moth and insect wings, egg cases, buds, feathers, seeds, leaf scars, moss, molds, ferns, common crystals, etc.—all with an ordinary, inexpensive magnifying glass. 209 exact line drawings aid in your discoveries. 220pp. 5⅜ × 8½. 23330-8 Pa. $4.50

RODIN ON ART AND ARTISTS, Auguste Rodin. Great sculptor's candid, wide-ranging comments on meaning of art; great artists; relation of sculpture to poetry, painting, music; philosophy of life, more. 76 superb black-and-white illustrations of Rodin's sculpture, drawings and prints. 119pp. 8⅜ × 11¼. 24487-3 Pa. $6.95

FIFTY CLASSIC FRENCH FILMS, 1912–1982: A Pictorial Record, Anthony Slide. Memorable stills from Grand Illusion, Beauty and the Beast, Hiroshima, Mon Amour, many more. Credits, plot synopses, reviews, etc. 160pp. 8¼ × 11. 25256-6 Pa. $11.95

THE PRINCIPLES OF PSYCHOLOGY, William James. Famous long course complete, unabridged. Stream of thought, time perception, memory, experimental methods; great work decades ahead of its time. 94 figures. 1,391pp. 5⅜ × 8½. 20381-6, 20382-4 Pa., Two-vol. set $19.90

BODIES IN A BOOKSHOP, R. T. Campbell. Challenging mystery of blackmail and murder with ingenious plot and superbly drawn characters. In the best tradition of British suspense fiction. 192pp. 5⅜ × 8½. 24720-1 Pa. $3.95

CALLAS: PORTRAIT OF A PRIMA DONNA, George Jellinek. Renowned commentator on the musical scene chronicles incredible career and life of the most controversial, fascinating, influential operatic personality of our time. 64 black-and-white photographs. 416pp. 5⅜ × 8¼. 25047-4 Pa. $7.95

GEOMETRY, RELATIVITY AND THE FOURTH DIMENSION, Rudolph Rucker. Exposition of fourth dimension, concepts of relativity as Flatland characters continue adventures. Popular, easily followed yet accurate, profound. 141 illustrations. 133pp. 5⅜ × 8½. 23400-2 Pa. $3.50

HOUSEHOLD STORIES BY THE BROTHERS GRIMM, with pictures by Walter Crane. 53 classic stories—Rumpelstiltskin, Rapunzel, Hansel and Gretel, the Fisherman and his Wife, Snow White, Tom Thumb, Sleeping Beauty, Cinderella, and so much more—lavishly illustrated with original 19th century drawings. 114 illustrations. x + 269pp. 5⅜ × 8½. 21080-4 Pa. $4.50

SUNDIALS, Albert Waugh. Far and away the best, most thorough coverage of ideas, mathematics concerned, types, construction, adjusting anywhere. Over 100 illustrations. 230pp. 5⅜ × 8½. 22947-5 Pa. $4.50

PICTURE HISTORY OF THE NORMANDIE: With 190 Illustrations, Frank O. Braynard. Full story of legendary French ocean liner: Art Deco interiors, design innovations, furnishings, celebrities, maiden voyage, tragic fire, much more. Extensive text. 144pp. 8⅜ × 11¾. 25257-4 Pa. $9.95

THE FIRST AMERICAN COOKBOOK: A Facsimile of "American Cookery," 1796, Amelia Simmons. Facsimile of the first American-written cookbook published in the United States contains authentic recipes for colonial favorites—pumpkin pudding, winter squash pudding, spruce beer, Indian slapjacks, and more. Introductory Essay and Glossary of colonial cooking terms. 80pp. 5⅜ × 8½. 24710-4 Pa. $3.50

101 PUZZLES IN THOUGHT AND LOGIC, C. R. Wylie, Jr. Solve murders and robberies, find out which fishermen are liars, how a blind man could possibly identify a color—purely by your own reasoning! 107pp. 5⅜ × 8½. 20367-0 Pa. $2.50

THE BOOK OF WORLD-FAMOUS MUSIC—CLASSICAL, POPULAR AND FOLK, James J. Fuld. Revised and enlarged republication of landmark work in musico-bibliography. Full information about nearly 1,000 songs and compositions including first lines of music and lyrics. New supplement. Index. 800pp. 5⅜ × 8¼. 24857-7 Pa. $14.95

ANTHROPOLOGY AND MODERN LIFE, Franz Boas. Great anthropologist's classic treatise on race and culture. Introduction by Ruth Bunzel. Only inexpensive paperback edition. 255pp. 5⅜ × 8½. 25245-0 Pa. $5.95

THE TALE OF PETER RABBIT, Beatrix Potter. The inimitable Peter's terrifying adventure in Mr. McGregor's garden, with all 27 wonderful, full-color Potter illustrations. 55pp. 4¼ × 5½. (Available in U.S. only) 22827-4 Pa. $1.75

THREE PROPHETIC SCIENCE FICTION NOVELS, H. G. Wells. *When the Sleeper Wakes, A Story of the Days to Come* and *The Time Machine* (full version). 335pp. 5⅜ × 8½. (Available in U.S. only) 20605-X Pa. $5.95

APICIUS COOKERY AND DINING IN IMPERIAL ROME, edited and translated by Joseph Dommers Vehling. Oldest known cookbook in existence offers readers a clear picture of what foods Romans ate, how they prepared them, etc. 49 illustrations. 301pp. 6⅛ × 9¼. 23563-7 Pa. $6.50

SHAKESPEARE LEXICON AND QUOTATION DICTIONARY, Alexander Schmidt. Full definitions, locations, shades of meaning of every word in plays and poems. More than 50,000 exact quotations. 1,485pp. 6½ × 9¼. 22726-X, 22727-8 Pa., Two-vol. set $27.90

THE WORLD'S GREAT SPEECHES, edited by Lewis Copeland and Lawrence W. Lamm. Vast collection of 278 speeches from Greeks to 1970. Powerful and effective models; unique look at history. 842pp. 5⅜ × 8½. 20468-5 Pa. $11.95

THE BLUE FAIRY BOOK, Andrew Lang. The first, most famous collection, with many familiar tales: Little Red Riding Hood, Aladdin and the Wonderful Lamp, Puss in Boots, Sleeping Beauty, Hansel and Gretel, Rumpelstiltskin; 37 in all. 138 illustrations. 390pp. 5⅜ × 8½. 21437-0 Pa. $5.95

THE STORY OF THE CHAMPIONS OF THE ROUND TABLE, Howard Pyle. Sir Launcelot, Sir Tristram and Sir Percival in spirited adventures of love and triumph retold in Pyle's inimitable style. 50 drawings, 31 full-page. xviii + 329pp. 6½ × 9¼. 21883-X Pa. $6.95

AUDUBON AND HIS JOURNALS, Maria Audubon. Unmatched two-volume portrait of the great artist, naturalist and author contains his journals, an excellent biography by his granddaughter, expert annotations by the noted ornithologist, Dr. Elliott Coues, and 37 superb illustrations. Total of 1,200pp. 5⅜ × 8.
Vol. I 25143-8 Pa. $8.95
Vol. II 25144-6 Pa. $8.95

GREAT DINOSAUR HUNTERS AND THEIR DISCOVERIES, Edwin H. Colbert. Fascinating, lavishly illustrated chronicle of dinosaur research, 1820's to 1960. Achievements of Cope, Marsh, Brown, Buckland, Mantell, Huxley, many others. 384pp. 5¼ × 8¼. 24701-5 Pa. $6.95

THE TASTEMAKERS, Russell Lynes. Informal, illustrated social history of American taste 1850's–1950's. First popularized categories Highbrow, Lowbrow, Middlebrow. 129 illustrations. New (1979) afterword. 384pp. 6 × 9.
23993-4 Pa. $6.95

DOUBLE CROSS PURPOSES, Ronald A. Knox. A treasure hunt in the Scottish Highlands, an old map, unidentified corpse, surprise discoveries keep reader guessing in this cleverly intricate tale of financial skullduggery. 2 black-and-white maps. 320pp. 5⅜ × 8½. (Available in U.S. only) 25032-6 Pa. $5.95

AUTHENTIC VICTORIAN DECORATION AND ORNAMENTATION IN FULL COLOR: 46 Plates from "Studies in Design," Christopher Dresser. Superb full-color lithographs reproduced from rare original portfolio of a major Victorian designer. 48pp. 9¼ × 12¼. 25083-0 Pa. $7.95

PRIMITIVE ART, Franz Boas. Remains the best text ever prepared on subject, thoroughly discussing Indian, African, Asian, Australian, and, especially, Northern American primitive art. Over 950 illustrations show ceramics, masks, totem poles, weapons, textiles, paintings, much more. 376pp. 5⅜ × 8. 20025-6 Pa. $6.95

SIDELIGHTS ON RELATIVITY, Albert Einstein. Unabridged republication of two lectures delivered by the great physicist in 1920–21. *Ether and Relativity* and *Geometry and Experience*. Elegant ideas in non-mathematical form, accessible to intelligent layman. vi + 56pp. 5⅜ × 8½. 24511-X Pa. $2.95

THE WIT AND HUMOR OF OSCAR WILDE, edited by Alvin Redman. More than 1,000 ripostes, paradoxes, wisecracks: Work is the curse of the drinking classes, I can resist everything except temptation, etc. 258pp. 5⅜ × 8½. 20602-5 Pa. $4.50

ADVENTURES WITH A MICROSCOPE, Richard Headstrom. 59 adventures with clothing fibers, protozoa, ferns and lichens, roots and leaves, much more. 142 illustrations. 232pp. 5⅜ × 8½. 23471-1 Pa. $3.95

PLANTS OF THE BIBLE, Harold N. Moldenke and Alma L. Moldenke. Standard reference to all 230 plants mentioned in Scriptures. Latin name, biblical reference, uses, modern identity, much more. Unsurpassed encyclopedic resource for scholars, botanists, nature lovers, students of Bible. Bibliography. Indexes. 123 black-and-white illustrations. 384pp. 6 × 9. 25069-5 Pa. $8.95

FAMOUS AMERICAN WOMEN: A Biographical Dictionary from Colonial Times to the Present, Robert McHenry, ed. From Pocahontas to Rosa Parks, 1,035 distinguished American women documented in separate biographical entries. Accurate, up-to-date data, numerous categories, spans 400 years. Indices. 493pp. 6½ × 9¼. 24523-3 Pa. $9.95

THE FABULOUS INTERIORS OF THE GREAT OCEAN LINERS IN HISTORIC PHOTOGRAPHS, William H. Miller, Jr. Some 200 superb photographs capture exquisite interiors of world's great "floating palaces"—1890's to 1980's: Titanic, Ile de France, Queen Elizabeth, United States, Europa, more. Approx. 200 black-and-white photographs. Captions. Text. Introduction. 160pp. 8⅜ × 11¼. 24756-2 Pa. $9.95

THE GREAT LUXURY LINERS, 1927-1954: A Photographic Record, William H. Miller, Jr. Nostalgic tribute to heyday of ocean liners. 186 photos of Ile de France, Normandie, Leviathan, Queen Elizabeth, United States, many others. Interior and exterior views. Introduction. Captions. 160pp. 9 × 12. 24056-8 Pa. $9.95

A NATURAL HISTORY OF THE DUCKS, John Charles Phillips. Great landmark of ornithology offers complete detailed coverage of nearly 200 species and subspecies of ducks: gadwall, sheldrake, merganser, pintail, many more. 74 full-color plates, 102 black-and-white. Bibliography. Total of 1,920pp. 8⅜ × 11¼. 25141-1, 25142-X Cloth. Two-vol. set $100.00

THE SEAWEED HANDBOOK: An Illustrated Guide to Seaweeds from North Carolina to Canada, Thomas F. Lee. Concise reference covers 78 species. Scientific and common names, habitat, distribution, more. Finding keys for easy identification. 224pp. 5⅜ × 8½. 25215-9 Pa. $5.95

THE TEN BOOKS OF ARCHITECTURE: The 1755 Leoni Edition, Leon Battista Alberti. Rare classic helped introduce the glories of ancient architecture to the Renaissance. 68 black-and-white plates. 336pp. 8⅜ × 11¼. 25239-6 Pa. $14.95

MISS MACKENZIE, Anthony Trollope. Minor masterpieces by Victorian master unmasks many truths about life in 19th-century England. First inexpensive edition in years. 392pp. 5⅜ × 8½. 25201-9 Pa. $7.95

THE RIME OF THE ANCIENT MARINER, Gustave Doré, Samuel Taylor Coleridge. Dramatic engravings considered by many to be his greatest work. The terrifying space of the open sea, the storms and whirlpools of an unknown ocean, the ice of Antarctica, more—all rendered in a powerful, chilling manner. Full text. 38 plates. 77pp. 9¼ × 12. 22305-1 Pa. $4.95

THE EXPEDITIONS OF ZEBULON MONTGOMERY PIKE, Zebulon Montgomery Pike. Fascinating first-hand accounts (1805-6) of exploration of Mississippi River, Indian wars, capture by Spanish dragoons, much more. 1,088pp. 5⅜ × 8½. 25254-X, 25255-8 Pa. Two-vol. set $23.90

CATALOG OF DOVER BOOKS

A CONCISE HISTORY OF PHOTOGRAPHY: Third Revised Edition, Helmut Gernsheim. Best one-volume history—camera obscura, photochemistry, daguerreotypes, evolution of cameras, film, more. Also artistic aspects—landscape, portraits, fine art, etc. 281 black-and-white photographs. 26 in color. 176pp. 8⅜ × 11¼. 25128-4 Pa. $12.95

THE DORÉ BIBLE ILLUSTRATIONS, Gustave Doré. 241 detailed plates from the Bible: the Creation scenes, Adam and Eve, Flood, Babylon, battle sequences, life of Jesus, etc. Each plate is accompanied by the verses from the King James version of the Bible. 241pp. 9 × 12. 23004-X Pa. $8.95

HUGGER-MUGGER IN THE LOUVRE, Elliot Paul. Second Homer Evans mystery-comedy. Theft at the Louvre involves sleuth in hilarious, madcap caper. "A knockout."—Books. 336pp. 5⅜ × 8½. 25185-3 Pa. $5.95

FLATLAND, E. A. Abbott. Intriguing and enormously popular science-fiction classic explores the complexities of trying to survive as a two-dimensional being in a three-dimensional world. Amusingly illustrated by the author. 16 illustrations. 103pp. 5⅜ × 8½. 20001-9 Pa. $2.25

THE HISTORY OF THE LEWIS AND CLARK EXPEDITION, Meriwether Lewis and William Clark, edited by Elliott Coues. Classic edition of Lewis and Clark's day-by-day journals that later became the basis for U.S. claims to Oregon and the West. Accurate and invaluable geographical, botanical, biological, meteorological and anthropological material. Total of 1,508pp. 5⅜ × 8½. 21268-8, 21269-6, 21270-X Pa. Three-vol. set $25.50

LANGUAGE, TRUTH AND LOGIC, Alfred J. Ayer. Famous, clear introduction to Vienna, Cambridge schools of Logical Positivism. Role of philosophy, elimination of metaphysics, nature of analysis, etc. 160pp. 5⅜ × 8½. (Available in U.S. and Canada only) 20010-8 Pa. $2.95

MATHEMATICS FOR THE NONMATHEMATICIAN, Morris Kline. Detailed, college-level treatment of mathematics in cultural and historical context, with numerous exercises. For liberal arts students. Preface. Recommended Reading Lists. Tables. Index. Numerous black-and-white figures. xvi + 641pp. 5⅜ × 8½. 24823-2 Pa. $11.95

28 SCIENCE FICTION STORIES, H. G. Wells. Novels, *Star Begotten* and *Men Like Gods*, plus 26 short stories: "Empire of the Ants," "A Story of the Stone Age," "The Stolen Bacillus," "In the Abyss," etc. 915pp. 5⅜ × 8½. (Available in U.S. only) 20265-8 Cloth. $10.95

HANDBOOK OF PICTORIAL SYMBOLS, Rudolph Modley. 3,250 signs and symbols, many systems in full; official or heavy commercial use. Arranged by subject. Most in Pictorial Archive series. 143pp. 8⅜ × 11. 23357-X Pa. $5.95

INCIDENTS OF TRAVEL IN YUCATAN, John L. Stephens. Classic (1843) exploration of jungles of Yucatan, looking for evidences of Maya civilization. Travel adventures, Mexican and Indian culture, etc. Total of 669pp. 5⅜ × 8½. 20926-1, 20927-X Pa., Two-vol. set $9.90

DEGAS: An Intimate Portrait, Ambroise Vollard. Charming, anecdotal memoir by famous art dealer of one of the greatest 19th-century French painters. 14 black-and-white illustrations. Introduction by Harold L. Van Doren. 96pp. 5⅜ × 8½.
25131-4 Pa. $3.95

PERSONAL NARRATIVE OF A PILGRIMAGE TO ALMANDINAH AND MECCAH, Richard Burton. Great travel classic by remarkably colorful personality. Burton, disguised as a Moroccan, visited sacred shrines of Islam, narrowly escaping death. 47 illustrations. 959pp. 5⅜ × 8½. 21217-3, 21218-1 Pa., Two-vol. set $17.90

PHRASE AND WORD ORIGINS, A. H. Holt. Entertaining, reliable, modern study of more than 1,200 colorful words, phrases, origins and histories. Much unexpected information. 254pp. 5⅜ × 8½. 20758-7 Pa. $5.95

THE RED THUMB MARK, R. Austin Freeman. In this first Dr. Thorndyke case, the great scientific detective draws fascinating conclusions from the nature of a single fingerprint. Exciting story, authentic science. 320pp. 5⅜ × 8½. (Available in U.S. only) 25210-8 Pa. $5.95

AN EGYPTIAN HIEROGLYPHIC DICTIONARY, E. A. Wallis Budge. Monumental work containing about 25,000 words or terms that occur in texts ranging from 3000 B.C. to 600 A.D. Each entry consists of a transliteration of the word, the word in hieroglyphs, and the meaning in English. 1,314pp. 6⅜ × 10.
23615-3, 23616-1 Pa., Two-vol. set $27.90

THE COMPLEAT STRATEGYST: Being a Primer on the Theory of Games of Strategy, J. D. Williams. Highly entertaining classic describes, with many illustrated examples, how to select best strategies in conflict situations. Prefaces. Appendices. xvi + 268pp. 5⅜ × 8½. 25101-2 Pa. $5.95

THE ROAD TO OZ, L. Frank Baum. Dorothy meets the Shaggy Man, little Button-Bright and the Rainbow's beautiful daughter in this delightful trip to the magical Land of Oz. 272pp. 5⅜ × 8. 25208-6 Pa. $4.95

POINT AND LINE TO PLANE, Wassily Kandinsky. Seminal exposition of role of point, line, other elements in non-objective painting. Essential to understanding 20th-century art. 127 illustrations. 192pp. 6½ × 9¼. 23808-3 Pa. $4.50

LADY ANNA, Anthony Trollope. Moving chronicle of Countess Lovel's bitter struggle to win for herself and daughter Anna their rightful rank and fortune—perhaps at cost of sanity itself. 384pp. 5⅜ × 8½. 24669-8 Pa. $6.95

EGYPTIAN MAGIC, E. A. Wallis Budge. Sums up all that is known about magic in Ancient Egypt: the role of magic in controlling the gods, powerful amulets that warded off evil spirits, scarabs of immortality, use of wax images, formulas and spells, the secret name, much more. 253pp. 5⅜ × 8½. 22681-6 Pa. $4.50

THE DANCE OF SIVA, Ananda Coomaraswamy. Preeminent authority unfolds the vast metaphysic of India: the revelation of her art, conception of the universe, social organization, etc. 27 reproductions of art masterpieces. 192pp. 5⅜ × 8½.
24817-8 Pa. $5.95

CHRISTMAS CUSTOMS AND TRADITIONS, Clement A. Miles. Origin, evolution, significance of religious, secular practices. Caroling, gifts, yule logs, much more. Full, scholarly yet fascinating; non-sectarian. 400pp. 5⅜ × 8½.
23354-5 Pa. $6.50

THE HUMAN FIGURE IN MOTION, Eadweard Muybridge. More than 4,500 stopped-action photos, in action series, showing undraped men, women, children jumping, lying down, throwing, sitting, wrestling, carrying, etc. 390pp. 7⅞ × 10⅝.
20204-6 Cloth. $19.95

THE MAN WHO WAS THURSDAY, Gilbert Keith Chesterton. Witty, fast-paced novel about a club of anarchists in turn-of-the-century London. Brilliant social, religious, philosophical speculations. 128pp. 5⅜ × 8½.
25121-7 Pa. $3.95

A CEZANNE SKETCHBOOK: Figures, Portraits, Landscapes and Still Lifes, Paul Cezanne. Great artist experiments with tonal effects, light, mass, other qualities in over 100 drawings. A revealing view of developing master painter, precursor of Cubism. 102 black-and-white illustrations. 144pp. 8¾ × 6⅝.
24790-2 Pa. $5.95

AN ENCYCLOPEDIA OF BATTLES: Accounts of Over 1,560 Battles from 1479 B.C. to the Present, David Eggenberger. Presents essential details of every major battle in recorded history, from the first battle of Megiddo in 1479 B.C. to Grenada in 1984. List of Battle Maps. New Appendix covering the years 1967–1984. Index. 99 illustrations. 544pp. 6½ × 9¼.
24913-1 Pa. $14.95

AN ETYMOLOGICAL DICTIONARY OF MODERN ENGLISH, Ernest Weekley. Richest, fullest work, by foremost British lexicographer. Detailed word histories. Inexhaustible. Total of 856pp. 6½ × 9¼.
21873-2, 21874-0 Pa., Two-vol. set $17.00

WEBSTER'S AMERICAN MILITARY BIOGRAPHIES, edited by Robert McHenry. Over 1,000 figures who shaped 3 centuries of American military history. Detailed biographies of Nathan Hale, Douglas MacArthur, Mary Hallaren, others. Chronologies of engagements, more. Introduction. Addenda. 1,033 entries in alphabetical order. xi + 548pp. 6½ × 9¼. (Available in U.S. only)
24758-9 Pa. $11.95

LIFE IN ANCIENT EGYPT, Adolf Erman. Detailed older account, with much not in more recent books: domestic life, religion, magic, medicine, commerce, and whatever else needed for complete picture. Many illustrations. 597pp. 5⅜ × 8½.
22632-8 Pa. $8.95

HISTORIC COSTUME IN PICTURES, Braun & Schneider. Over 1,450 costumed figures shown, covering a wide variety of peoples: kings, emperors, nobles, priests, servants, soldiers, scholars, townsfolk, peasants, merchants, courtiers, cavaliers, and more. 256pp. 8⅜ × 11¼.
23150-X Pa. $7.95

THE NOTEBOOKS OF LEONARDO DA VINCI, edited by J. P. Richter. Extracts from manuscripts reveal great genius; on painting, sculpture, anatomy, sciences, geography, etc. Both Italian and English. 186 ms. pages reproduced, plus 500 additional drawings, including studies for *Last Supper*, *Sforza* monument, etc. 860pp. 7⅞ × 10¾. (Available in U.S. only) 22572-0, 22573-9 Pa., Two-vol. set $25.90

THE ART NOUVEAU STYLE BOOK OF ALPHONSE MUCHA: All 72 Plates from "Documents Decoratifs" in Original Color, Alphonse Mucha. Rare copyright-free design portfolio by high priest of Art Nouveau. Jewelry, wallpaper, stained glass, furniture, figure studies, plant and animal motifs, etc. Only complete one-volume edition. 80pp. 9⅜ × 12¼. 24044-4 Pa. $8.95

ANIMALS: 1,419 COPYRIGHT-FREE ILLUSTRATIONS OF MAMMALS, BIRDS, FISH, INSECTS, ETC., edited by Jim Harter. Clear wood engravings present, in extremely lifelike poses, over 1,000 species of animals. One of the most extensive pictorial sourcebooks of its kind. Captions. Index. 284pp. 9 × 12. 23766-4 Pa. $9.95

OBELISTS FLY HIGH, C. Daly King. Masterpiece of American detective fiction, long out of print, involves murder on a 1935 transcontinental flight—"a very thrilling story"—NY Times. Unabridged and unaltered republication of the edition published by William Collins Sons & Co. Ltd., London, 1935. 288pp. 5⅜ × 8½. (Available in U.S. only) 25036-9 Pa. $4.95

VICTORIAN AND EDWARDIAN FASHION: A Photographic Survey, Alison Gernsheim. First fashion history completely illustrated by contemporary photographs. Full text plus 235 photos, 1840–1914, in which many celebrities appear. 240pp. 6½ × 9¼. 24205-6 Pa. $6.00

THE ART OF THE FRENCH ILLUSTRATED BOOK, 1700–1914, Gordon N. Ray. Over 630 superb book illustrations by Fragonard, Delacroix, Daumier, Doré, Grandville, Manet, Mucha, Steinlen, Toulouse-Lautrec and many others. Preface. Introduction. 633 halftones. Indices of artists, authors & titles, binders and provenances. Appendices. Bibliography. 608pp. 8⅜ × 11¼. 25086-5 Pa. $24.95

THE WONDERFUL WIZARD OF OZ, L. Frank Baum. Facsimile in full color of America's finest children's classic. 143 illustrations by W. W. Denslow. 267pp. 5⅜ × 8½. 20691-2 Pa. $5.95

FRONTIERS OF MODERN PHYSICS: New Perspectives on Cosmology, Relativity, Black Holes and Extraterrestrial Intelligence, Tony Rothman, et al. For the intelligent layman. Subjects include: cosmological models of the universe; black holes; the neutrino; the search for extraterrestrial intelligence. Introduction. 46 black-and-white illustrations. 192pp. 5⅜ × 8½. 24587-X Pa. $6.95

THE FRIENDLY STARS, Martha Evans Martin & Donald Howard Menzel. Classic text marshalls the stars together in an engaging, non-technical survey, presenting them as sources of beauty in night sky. 23 illustrations. Foreword. 2 star charts. Index. 147pp. 5⅜ × 8½. 21099-5 Pa. $3.50

FADS AND FALLACIES IN THE NAME OF SCIENCE, Martin Gardner. Fair, witty appraisal of cranks, quacks, and quackeries of science and pseudoscience: hollow earth, Velikovsky, orgone energy, Dianetics, flying saucers, Bridey Murphy, food and medical fads, etc. Revised, expanded In the Name of Science. "A very able and even-tempered presentation."—The New Yorker. 363pp. 5⅜ × 8. 20394-8 Pa. $6.50

ANCIENT EGYPT: ITS CULTURE AND HISTORY, J. E Manchip White. From pre-dynastics through Ptolemies: society, history, political structure, religion, daily life, literature, cultural heritage. 48 plates. 217pp. 5⅜ × 8½. 22548-8 Pa. $4.95

SIR HARRY HOTSPUR OF HUMBLETHWAITE, Anthony Trollope. Incisive, unconventional psychological study of a conflict between a wealthy baronet, his idealistic daughter, and their scapegrace cousin. The 1870 novel in its first inexpensive edition in years. 250pp. 5⅜ × 8½. 24953-0 Pa. $5.95

LASERS AND HOLOGRAPHY, Winston E. Kock. Sound introduction to burgeoning field, expanded (1981) for second edition. Wave patterns, coherence, lasers, diffraction, zone plates, properties of holograms, recent advances. 84 illustrations. 160pp. 5⅜ × 8¼. (Except in United Kingdom) 24041-X Pa. $3.50

INTRODUCTION TO ARTIFICIAL INTELLIGENCE: SECOND, EN-LARGED EDITION, Philip C. Jackson, Jr. Comprehensive survey of artificial intelligence—the study of how machines (computers) can be made to act intelligently. Includes introductory and advanced material. Extensive notes updating the main text. 132 black-and-white illustrations. 512pp. 5⅜ × 8½. 24864-X Pa. $8.95

HISTORY OF INDIAN AND INDONESIAN ART, Ananda K. Coomaraswamy. Over 400 illustrations illuminate classic study of Indian art from earliest Harappa finds to early 20th century. Provides philosophical, religious and social insights. 304pp. 6⅜ × 9⅜. 25005-9 Pa. $8.95

THE GOLEM, Gustav Meyrink. Most famous supernatural novel in modern European literature, set in Ghetto of Old Prague around 1890. Compelling story of mystical experiences, strange transformations, profound terror. 13 black-and-white illustrations. 224pp. 5⅜ × 8½. (Available in U.S. only) 25025-3 Pa. $5.95

ARMADALE, Wilkie Collins. Third great mystery novel by the author of *The Woman in White* and *The Moonstone*. Original magazine version with 40 illustrations. 597pp. 5⅜ × 8½. 23429-0 Pa. $9.95

PICTORIAL ENCYCLOPEDIA OF HISTORIC ARCHITECTURAL PLANS, DETAILS AND ELEMENTS: With 1,880 Line Drawings of Arches, Domes, Doorways, Facades, Gables, Windows, etc., John Theodore Haneman. Sourcebook of inspiration for architects, designers, others. Bibliography. Captions. 141pp. 9 × 12. 24605-1 Pa. $6.95

BENCHLEY LOST AND FOUND, Robert Benchley. Finest humor from early 30's, about pet peeves, child psychologists, post office and others. Mostly unavailable elsewhere. 73 illustrations by Peter Arno and others. 183pp. 5⅜ × 8½. 22410-4 Pa. $3.95

ERTÉ GRAPHICS, Erté. Collection of striking color graphics: *Seasons, Alphabet, Numerals, Aces* and *Precious Stones*. 50 plates, including 4 on covers. 48pp. 9⅜ × 12¼. 23580-7 Pa. $6.95

THE JOURNAL OF HENRY D. THOREAU, edited by Bradford Torrey, F. H. Allen. Complete reprinting of 14 volumes, 1837–61, over two million words; the sourcebooks for *Walden*, etc. Definitive. All original sketches, plus 75 photographs. 1,804pp. 8½ × 12¼. 20312-3, 20313-1 Cloth., Two-vol. set $80.00

CASTLES: THEIR CONSTRUCTION AND HISTORY, Sidney Toy. Traces castle development from ancient roots. Nearly 200 photographs and drawings illustrate moats, keeps, baileys, many other features. Caernarvon, Dover Castles, Hadrian's Wall, Tower of London, dozens more. 256pp. 5⅜ × 8¼. 24898-4 Pa. $5.95

AMERICAN CLIPPER SHIPS: 1833–1858, Octavius T. Howe & Frederick C. Matthews. Fully-illustrated, encyclopedic review of 352 clipper ships from the period of America's greatest maritime supremacy. Introduction. 109 halftones. 5 black-and-white line illustrations. Index. Total of 928pp. 5⅜ × 8½.
25115-2, 25116-0 Pa., Two-vol. set $17.90

TOWARDS A NEW ARCHITECTURE, Le Corbusier. Pioneering manifesto by great architect, near legendary founder of "International School." Technical and aesthetic theories, views on industry, economics, relation of form to function, "mass-production spirit," much more. Profusely illustrated. Unabridged translation of 13th French edition. Introduction by Frederick Etchells. 320pp. 6⅛ × 9¼. (Available in U.S. only)
25023-7 Pa. $8.95

THE BOOK OF KELLS, edited by Blanche Cirker. Inexpensive collection of 32 full-color, full-page plates from the greatest illuminated manuscript of the Middle Ages, painstakingly reproduced from rare facsimile edition. Publisher's Note. Captions. 32pp. 9⅜ × 12¼.
24345-1 Pa. $4.95

BEST SCIENCE FICTION STORIES OF H. G. WELLS, H. G. Wells. Full novel *The Invisible Man,* plus 17 short stories: "The Crystal Egg," "Aepyornis Island," "The Strange Orchid," etc. 303pp. 5⅜ × 8½. (Available in U.S. only)
21531-8 Pa. $4.95

AMERICAN SAILING SHIPS: Their Plans and History, Charles G. Davis. Photos, construction details of schooners, frigates, clippers, other sailcraft of 18th to early 20th centuries—plus entertaining discourse on design, rigging, nautical lore, much more. 137 black-and-white illustrations. 240pp. 6⅛ × 9¼.
24658-2 Pa. $5.95

ENTERTAINING MATHEMATICAL PUZZLES, Martin Gardner. Selection of author's favorite conundrums involving arithmetic, money, speed, etc., with lively commentary. Complete solutions. 112pp. 5⅜ × 8½.
25211-6 Pa. $2.95

THE WILL TO BELIEVE, HUMAN IMMORTALITY, William James. Two books bound together. Effect of irrational on logical, and arguments for human immortality. 402pp. 5⅜ × 8½.
20291-7 Pa. $7.50

THE HAUNTED MONASTERY and THE CHINESE MAZE MURDERS, Robert Van Gulik. 2 full novels by Van Gulik continue adventures of Judge Dee and his companions. An evil Taoist monastery, seemingly supernatural events; overgrown topiary maze that hides strange crimes. Set in 7th-century China. 27 illustrations. 328pp. 5⅜ × 8½.
23502-5 Pa. $5.95

CELEBRATED CASES OF JUDGE DEE (DEE GOONG AN), translated by Robert Van Gulik. Authentic 18th-century Chinese detective novel; Dee and associates solve three interlocked cases. Led to Van Gulik's own stories with same characters. Extensive introduction. 9 illustrations. 237pp. 5⅜ × 8½.
23337-5 Pa. $4.95

Prices subject to change without notice.

Available at your book dealer or write for free catalog to Dept. GI, Dover Publications, Inc., 31 East 2nd St., Mineola, N.Y. 11501. Dover publishes more than 175 books each year on science, elementary and advanced mathematics, biology, music, art, literary history, social sciences and other areas.